# ATIA

## BRONZE AGE WARRIOR

AN EPIC NOVEL
BOOK ONE OF THE
BRONZE AGE WARRIOR SERIES

AN ORIGINAL STORY BY
BUD SELIGSON

LOST AGE PUBLISHING

—2017—

ATIA: BRONZE AGE WARRIOR © 2015 Bud Seligson

The following original novel has been filed and registered with the Writers' Guild of America, West, under the name of Bud Seligson.

Printed in the United States of America

Edited by Beth Schindler
Cover Art and Interior design by: Cyrusfiction Productions.

ISBN: 978-1-946480-00-2

9018 Balboa Boulevard
Suite #562
Northridge, CA 91325

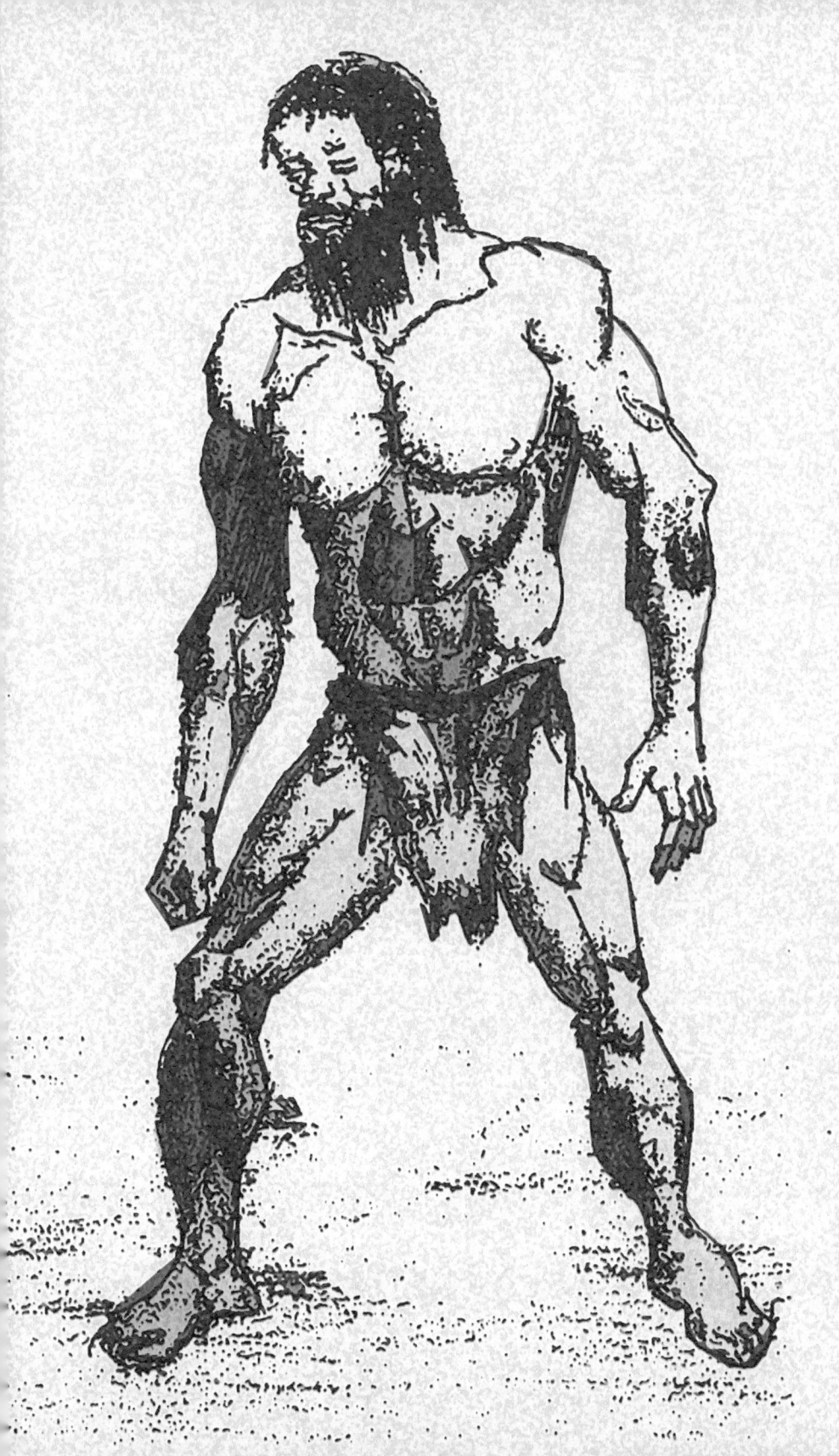

# DEDICATIONS

To my wife Diane,

If I listed all the many ways that you have helped me, this dedication would be larger than the novel.

—all my love, Bud

Also, to my editor, Beth Schlindler,

I would like to thank you for making my words flow.

# ATIA—BRONZE AGE WARRIOR

## FOREWORD

If this true story is about "Ötzi the Iceman", a scientific celebrity who was found perfectly preserved in the mountains of central Europe, then why is this novel being called "Atia, the Bronze Age warrior" and not "Ötzi"?

The answer is a simple one. Rather than fight in the court systems of Austria and Italy, we have decided to change the name of our hero, but to keep the facts of his adventurous life intact.

We therefore offer for your enjoyment, all the sword fights, passionate love affairs and early human-Neanderthal conflicts being fought for the ownership of the land.

This is a combination work of fact and fiction woven together as a product of the author's imagination.

What we have here is a riddle wrapped in a mystery inside of an enigma.

I would like to try to open the door to a time long ago and attempt to reveal an age of wonder and danger at the dawn of our ancestors who were the first modern humans.

We should all be aware that the label we have given ourselves, "homo sapiens" means "man the wise."

We must wonder, sometimes, about the accuracy of this label.

# Warning!

This novel is a really hot, sexual book with lots of violence. It contains sexually explicit scenes.

—Bud Seligson

# INTRODUCTION

# ATIA–THE ICEMAN: A SAGA FEATURING MOG–THE NEANDERTHAL

This is a dark age, a very bloody age—an age of violence and great love-making.

It is a land of giant mountains, mighty rivers, icy landscapes, and dark forests.

From their enigmatic beginnings through their first tests as warriors and leaders, some 5,300 years ago, both Atia, a human, and Mog, a Neanderthal, hold the destiny of the world in their capable hands.

Studies show that DNA from the extinct species of Neanderthal is evident in many people living in today's world.

᛭ ᛁᛁᛁᛏ ᚻᛏᛏ

The following is a partial word-for-word copy of the *Los Angeles Times* article written by ace reporter Geoffrey Mohan:

## "NEANDERTHAL DNA LIVES ON IN MODERN HUMANS ...

"The ancestors of most modern humans mated with Neanderthals and made off with important swaths of DNA that helped them adapt to new environments, scientists reported....

"Some of the genes gained from these trysts linger in people of European and east Asian descent, though many others were wiped out by natural selection, according to reports published ... by the journals *Nature* and *Science*.

"The stretches of Neanderthal DNA that remain include genes that altered hair and pigment, as well as others that strengthened the immune system, the scientists wrote. Together, they offer intriguing hints about how Neanderthal genes may have helped humans adapt as they spread around the globe.

"They also add to evidence that Neanderthals linger in us, about 30,000 years after they mysteriously vanished.

"'(Neanderthals) are not fully extinct, if you will,' said geneticist Svante Paabro of the Max Planck Institute for Evolutionary Anthropology in Leipzig, Germany ...'They live on in some of us today—a little bit.'

"Genes controlling keratin, a key component in the development of skin and hair, stand out as the strongest Neanderthal signal in a modern genome, Paabro said. Precisely how these may have helped change modern physical characteristics remains unresolved, (Paabo) added.

"The new studies confirm earlier findings that modern humans did more than bump elbows with Neanderthals when they encountered them after they left Africa.

"An estimated 1% to 3% of the human genome comes from Neanderthals, suggesting that members of the two species mated perhaps 300 times about 50,000 years ago, said Joshua M. Akey, a population geneticist from the University of Washington and a lead author of the study published in *Science*. There's no way to tell whether those encounters happened about the same time or were spread out over many generations, (Akey) said.

"The genetic signature of Neanderthals is slightly larger among east Asians. To Akey, that suggests a second wave of mating (occurred) after they parted from the forebears of Europeans. 'It's a two-night-stand theory now', he said."

⊤ �III⸍ ⸍⸍⊤

The author, Bud Seligson, wishes to add the results of two important findings that have recently come to light.

1. Based upon the scientific viewpoint, it is believed that these two groups of humanoids resulted when the early human females were captured by their enemies, the Neanderthals. The women were probably raped in the normal course of daily life and kept as slaves by their new masters.

The babies that the human females delivered definitely had many of the characteristics of Neanderthal fathers. We must assume that these cross bred children would have been taller and stronger than the original humans, who rarely grew to five and a half feet in height. This interbreeding probably gave female offspring the ability to have permanently larger breasts than their contemporary human females.

It is well known as an established fact that early human females were being depicted by scientists as having been very flat chested.

It is important to remember that early man was basically no different from our modern man of today in that girls with bigger breasts, or boobs, the slang word we use today, got more attention and probably got pregnant more often than the smaller-chested females.

Large-breasted women have always been more attractive to the male of the species and, therefore, in prehistoric times they were chosen as their mates. We personally believe that this theory still holds true today.

2. The second theory, which our scientists consider as possibly true, is the belief that early human beings were much more aggressive than the bigger and slower-moving Neanderthals.
It is firmly believed that humans hunted down Neanderthals with the humans' advanced invention of the bow and arrow. The entire line of Neanderthals was completely wiped out as a result.

'T' III' ʰT'T

An additional note from the author:

We need a moment here for a definition of what the Neanderthal was. The following is a statement taken directly from *Webster's New World Dictionary — Third College Edition*.

1. Designating a widespread form of early human called *Homo sapiens neanderthalensis* whose skeletal remains were first found in the Neander valley of European Germany;

2. A crude or primitive form of early man, thought to have been quite intelligent, who completely disappeared just about the same time as modern man (homo sapiens) began to appear;

3. A form of early man who completely disappeared by either interbreeding with, or being hunted out of existence by, early modern man;

4. A shorter and more powerful form of early man who disappeared

completely with the onset of early modern man.

They were thought to be more passive than the aggressive modern man and, with their lack of better tools and weapons of war, were completely replaced as rulers of the world.

*And now our story begins ...*

# THE SAGA OF ATIA, THE BRONZE AGE WARRIOR, AND MOG, THE NEANDERTHAL

## CHAPTER ONE

The two spears shimmered brightly in the moonlight as they clashed together, shattering the stillness of the quiet night with clangs of flint spearheads coming up against each other. Loud grunts and huge gusts of breath were wrenched from the sweaty throats of the two combatants.

A subdued murmur of sounds was evident from the circle of Neanderthal warriors who were gathered around the two fighters as they moved about within the circle created by the onlookers.

The only thing in common about the two men, who were fighting there, was the deadly skill with which each man wielded his spear.

There was one who was increasingly aggressive and was clearly the stronger of the two. His dexterous spear play indicated that the long straight spear was no stranger to his huge hands. He had a broad face with the accompanying high cheekbones and a thin small mouth beneath the bony ridges that overviewed his eyes. His ugly face was completed by a receding chin and unusually prominent teeth.

His opponent, much smaller in size and weight but equally skilled in the use of the weapons, was known as Atia, the leader of a small band of human hunters, who had carelessly blundered into the camp of one of the few remaining groups of Neanderthals still alive at this late date in evolution.

For tens of thousands of years, the Neanderthals had wandered about the local lands as hunters and gatherers. They never stayed in one place very long as they went about their daily lives. The Neanderthal tribes traveled over the plains, forests and mountains of Northern and Western Eurasia.

During the middle of the last Ice Age, about 30,000 years ago, a new type of being began to proliferate into the world of the Neanderthals. We call these new people early modern *Homo sapiens*, or modern man.

Amazingly, for all these many thousands of years, our world had two very different types of beings living their very separate lives. They competed with each other for living space and the various wild animals that they both hunted and needed for their survival.

The older, stronger Neanderthals were shorter than modern man and had greater musculatures. Their brains were as large as ours and perhaps even a little larger, though they were proportioned differently. The Neanderthals' brains were much smaller in front, therefore, they had visibly receding foreheads.

Scientists tell us that it is the frontal part of the brain that is associated with the rarer regions of abstract thought. They say that this was the reason that the Neanderthals, who were quite smart, were definitely not as smart as humans. Another way to put this into proper prospective is to say that modern-day man/*Homo sapiens* would score a 10 (the highest-ranking score on a scale of 1 to 10) in brain power, and the average Neanderthal would score about a 6+. At the time of Atia, only a few thousand Neanderthals were alive and still roaming the European lands.

Whenever a Neanderthal and a human met, one or the other did not usually walk away from the encounter.

On this occasion Atia and his men were chasing an antelope when they accidently blundered into the well -hidden campsite of the Neanderthals. The humans were easily overcome by the bigger and stronger beasts.

Atia, who had shown great courage and fighting skill in that very brief but violent encounter against the overwhelming force of the Neanderthal hunters, was stripped of his weapons and tied up to wait upon the pleasure of the Neanderthal leader, who called himself Jar.

Atia was told that Jar was going to engage him in a one-on-one battle with spears to see who the better man was. They told him that it was a great honor among their people to fight in a contest of skills with long spears.

If Atia defeated the huge leader of the Neanderthals in this battle to the death, then he would be set free. The Neanderthal leader laughed loudly as he told Atia about this upcoming contest of arms.

Atia was then tied to a huge wooden stake that had been driven into the ground off to the side of a huge fire that blazed brightly against the rapidly falling darkness.

Atia was not bothered again or even spoken to as the Neanderthals went about gathering together the weapons and personal belongings of the slain humans, who were simply dragged over to the far side of the campsite and then dumped into a large pile. They were left there for the animals of the night to feast upon after the Neanderthals moved to a different camp.

There was laughter and pounding of chests among the huge Neanderthals as they finished their meal around their large campfire. There was also much pointing of fingers at the tied-up human who was going to be the evening's entertainment.

Atia slid down the wooden pole and sat almost comfortably

even though his hands were tied behind him. He had been in many dangerous situations like this one in his forty-seven years of life and he had always survived. He planned on surviving this one, too.

Time passed slowly and finally the sleeping Atia was untied and allowed enough time for the circulation in his arms to return to normal so that he could fight the leader while he was at full strength.

There were several spears, which all appeared to be equal, and so he selected one of them at random.

He was then led into the fighting area where Jar, the Neanderthal leader, was waiting for him with a huge smile on his ugly face.

It wasn't long until a full circle of Neanderthals surrounded the two of them as they walked around a bit to loosen up their muscles in preparation for the fight. They each held a razor-sharp spear in their hands.

Upon closer examination, streaks of gray highlighted Atia's smooth black hair and his closely trimmed beard. He was in his forties in age and, due to the hard and always dangerous life that he had been forced to live, he was in top condition. He would be more than able to give a good account of himself in the duel to the death that was now getting ready to start.

It was an interesting fact that it had been many years since an opponent's weapon had touched Atia's face. His skill with weapons was talked about far and wide.

The onlooking Neanderthals were absolutely astonished as they watched the two combatants, who seemed to be equally skilled with their weapons.

The gathered Neanderthals were looking for an easy and quick finish to the fight and were very surprised at the skill being shown by the smaller human. Their knowing eyes missed nothing of the marvelous skill with the spear that was playing out in front of them.

The continued excitement was much too intense for any vocal comments from the crowd, and so they just stood there in complete silence as they continued to watch.

The two warriors were beginning to draw upon the limits of their strength. Each one watched the other for a sign showing weakness that would cause. his opponent to make a fatal mistake.

Both dueling spears had lately tasted blood.

A shallow gash of no consequence leaked across the bigger man's forearm where Atia's spear had cut across and lightly touched him.

Atia was bleeding slowly from a pair of slashes along his left side and from a deeper wound below his shoulder, which seemed to have crippled his left arm somewhat. He had received that wound when he had fought off three deadly thrusts that would have pierced his heart if his reflexes had been a fraction of a second slower.

Perhaps it was the flow of blood from Atia that prompted the thin smile and flared nostrils on the face of the Neanderthal as he confidently pressed in for the kill.

There was no smile on Atia's face, only anger that blazed brightly in his eyes. He refused to show any outward sign of the pain and fatigue that he was feeling.

Again, their spears darted, engaged, broke apart.

Not pausing in his relentless attack, the bigger man struck again even as their spears disengaged. The Neanderthal let the momentum of their brief exchange drive his flint-spear tip into the thick muscles of Atia's shoulder, where the forward edge of the tip broke off inside the smaller man's skin.

Atia grunted in agony, lunging backward from the blow. His legs buckled under him as he staggered, barely able to hold himself erect. His desperate counterthrust was extremely clumsy and completely without any strength behind it.

It had become the final moments of the duel.

The surrounding eyes of the crowd burned with breathless concentration.

The huge Neanderthal leader, playing to his adoring crowd of onlookers, was greatly enjoying the attention that was completely focused on him.

He decided that he was going to dispatch Atia with one of his blinding thrusts to the heart. This move had become his trademark over the years, and he knew that the move would be well received by his large audience.

Atia, who was most carefully watching his enemy, had absolutely no thought of good form. From his half -crouched position, he slashed upward, gripping the long hilt of his spear with both of his hands for added strength. The sharpened point of his spear caught the unprepared bigger man in his crotch and continued upward.

Poised to deliver his own deathblow against Atia, the big Neanderthal was flung back in a welter of spilling organs and burst lungs.

A long gasp of disbelief followed by a confused outburst of noise came from the shocked crowd.

The big man on the ground shuddered in a final spasm. His death rattle was drowned out by the excited shouts and curses that erupted from the crowd.

Atia put the bloody point of his spear to the ground and leaned hard against its hilt as he struggled to his feet. Blood was flowing slowly but steadily from his shoulder wound, but he made no outcry other than a hoarse gulping for breath.

He was very aware that as soon as the shock passed, the band of Neanderthal warriors would be all over him.

He quickly grabbed his weapons, which were lying nearby, and fled toward the nearby mountains. It was his hope that the approaching snowstorm would allow him to escape his enemies.

# CHAPTER TWO

Atia flew from his mortal enemies and headed straight up into the extremely high mountains of the Alps that surrounded the entire area.

As he climbed upward, the cold became so bitter that it felt like his skin was burning, but he did not hesitate, nor did he slow down.

He knew that his enemies were relentless trackers, and that his own hope of survival was to flee directly into the storm that was now bearing down on him.

He crouched against the raging wind with the snow flying in his face. The ground was covered with ice amid heavy banks of white, making it difficult for him to move forward.

The wind howled and roared.

He could feel his face freezing as he squinted his eyes to slits against the snow that pelted him like so many stinging darts.

Stumbling, sliding, stooping low against the biting wind, he groped toward the only protection that he could find—a looming snowbank that reared up massively in the bewildering blizzard of white. He sank down a bit and leaned his back against its protection.

The cold was inescapable but at least he was being sheltered from the slashing force of the wind.

He knew he had to find something that would get him out of

the weather, but what? The snow simply blanketed everything. Atia could not even tell where the horizon might be. Everything was completely blurred in the endless snow and ice.

He trudged through drifts that almost reached up to his armpits.

All feeling had left his cheeks, his ears, and his nose, but he could take in air through his lungs, and so he pushed on, hour after hour, growing hungrier and weaker with each painful, plodding step. The spearhead in his shoulder ached terribly.

The storm did not let up in the slightest. If anything, it seemed to be growing in strength, but through the swirling snow, he began to make out the dim gray form of something massive. He could finally see that it was a looming cliff of ice and rock scoured clean of snow by the furious wind. It jutted up stubbornly from the snow banked landscape standing jagged, raw, and dark against the gray and snowy sky.

He continued floundering through deep drifts, stopping only to breathe deeply, as his strength was ebbing fast.

All that he really wanted to do was to lie down and rest for a while in the soft snow, but he knew that if he did so, he would never get up.

Finally, he saw ahead a dark cleft in the rock. It was a cave, and he plunged ahead, using up the last of his failing energy.

The storm had created snowbanks around the base of the cliff in the forms of smooth-sliding ramps of white. He slid down one of them, slipping on the ice, until he was able to stagger up to the welcoming darkness offered by the cave's interior.

From inside the cave he saw that the snow had finally stopped. It was knee-high just outside the cave entrance where he was standing, but farther off it had drifted many feet deep.

The worst of the storm was over. The gray clouds were suddenly dashing along the skyline as if in a hurry to get away. The sun would soon be trying to break through.

Atia decided to rest for a little while inside the cave before he moved on.

Whenever he had free time, as he did now, Atia would push his memory way back in time to when he was only a young fellow trying to get along in a harsh world. He enjoyed reliving his memories from the past.

# THE AUSTRIAN/ITALIAN MOUNTAIN RANGE ABOUT THIRTY YEARS EARLIER

## CHAPTER THREE

Seven arrows left. Atia counted them one more time as he continued running.

He knew that there were at least twenty of *them* following him along his back trail.

Laughing out loud to himself, he realized that in order to clean up and get rid of his persistent Neanderthal trailers, all he had to do was kill three of them with each one of the seven arrows that he had left. If he did that, then everything would be just fine. He continued to laugh at his own grim sense of humor.

A tight smile curved his lips as he notched another arrow into his bow.

"I'll be lucky if I hit one with every third arrow," he said to himself out loud. He threw a quick glance over his shoulder as he continued to run down a narrow flat valley.

As always, one or two of those bastards were out in front of the pack, driving him on while the rest of them hung back in a large clump of moving bodies.

His trailers always seemed ready to move quickly to the right or left as he did whenever he changed direction. No matter what he did, he could not seem to shake them off of his tail.

When these deadly enemies first picked up his track, they had tried to stay close on his heels, probably assuming that he would wear out quickly so that they could close in on him for the final kill.

Atia got them to change their minds pretty quickly when four of his arrows had slashed into them in rapid succession. Each one of his arrows had found an easy target in the closely-packed mass of Neanderthal bodies.

They had dropped back out of his arrow range for a while as they continued chasing him. Atia knew that they were just waiting for him to tire out.

That had been early this morning. Now, many hours later, he was still running strongly as the sun began to set somewhere in the far distance.

Atia noticed that one of the Neanderthals was getting a bit careless as he was trying to gain a few yards on him. The big guy was probably hoping to get within better range of Atia so that he could throw one of his deadly spears at him.

Atia tightened his firm grip on his bow slowing down his rapid pace ever so slightly.

He took another look over his shoulder at the big man-thing that was chasing him. Just a few feet more, he thought, and the huge Neanderthal would be in perfect bow range for him. He carefully estimated the distance that his arrow would have to travel to hit his target.

The Neanderthals, as a group, were very good with their spears. Their everyday weapons were fairly short and slender, but they had long and very sharp tips that were shaped like leaves.

These "beast men," as Atia's people called the Neanderthals, were able to throw their weapons much farther than Atia had thought they could. They also surprised him with much greater accuracy than he had believed possible.

One minor scratch on his right side and a long shallow cut on his left leg had taught him an important lesson where their skill level was concerned.

This was the first personal contact that Atia, now in his late teens, had ever had with the Neanderthals.

Atia's tribe was seeing less and less of them moving about the mountain areas that they both shared.

Atia's people, whom we now call *Homo sapiens*, were seeing a great increase in their own people's population growth. The Neanderthals, however, seemed to be unable to adjust to the warming climate happening worldwide, or to the competition that Atia's people gave them on all fronts, especially with their weapons. All of these thoughts were running through Atia's head as he checked his two wounds.

He knew he had been very lucky that those thrown spears hadn't hit him straight on, and since he knew that he could not expect to be so lucky again, he was being very careful to keep running at a distance out of the throwing range of his pursuers.

Atia filled his lungs and let the air out with a loud sigh. The first of his eager pursuers was just about within bow range.

Another few steps and then Atia whirled around suddenly, planted his feet firmly, and shot off his arrow. The arrow sped true, catching the large, dark man squarely in the chest.

With a scream, the Neanderthal flung up his arms and quickly tumbled to the ground. Not waiting to see the results of his shot, Atia spun around and dashed off again.

His pursuers gave a great howl of rage as their comrade fell, but so intent were they on getting to Atia that not one of them stopped to check on the fallen warrior.

Time continued to pass, and it was just before the sun was getting ready to set that Atia realized he was no longer being chased. The Neanderthals must have decided to either stop their chase, or they were going to rest until morning and then pick up his trail again.

Either option was fine with Atia. He welcomed the much-needed rest as he slowed his pace down to a fast walk.

# CHAPTER FOUR

After outrunning his enemies, Atia was happy just to sit quietly by his small night fire.

He was spending his time doing what any warrior does whenever he has idle moments—repairing some of his gear and taking small catnaps.

His latest nap, however, did not last very long, nor was it very deep, for no sooner did he approach the realm of sleep when his usual sense of curiosity welled up inside him and brought him back to complete wakefulness. Atia was thinking about his personal desire to find out everything that there was to know about the wonderful world around him.

There was so much that Atia, whose brain was the equal of today's modern man, could have absorbed if only the information were out there, but he lived in a primitive society and he had little knowledge available to him.

His quest for knowledge was never to be satisfied for the rest of his entire life.

He wanted to understand why the sun would rise up each day, and why the moon would shine so brightly on some nights and not so much on others? Why did the stars look so cold, and why did the clouds look like rabbits and other familiar things? Why did rain fall? His questions just seemed to go on and on...

As a small child, his favorite word was always "why?" He would ask the questions of his tribal elders, but somehow they could never satisfy him with the answers.

The hours of the long night passed slowly as Atia sat by his dying fire.

He suddenly jumped up to get something to eat out of his pack and that quick movement actually saved his life. A hard-thrown spear thudded into the tree where he had been sitting. The spear vibrated violently with the force of the throw.

Instantly dropping to the ground, Atia rolled over and over swiftly trying to become a hard target to hit in case his attacker was planning to throw another spear at him. He finally stopped his rolling as he came upon a large bush that would cover him.

Atia came to his feet with his knife in his hand, ready to do battle and defend his life.

The big man thing charged at Atia with a wicked smile on his huge face.

He was sure that he would have no problem with the much-smaller man in the upcoming one-on-one knife fight.

The look on Atia's enemy's face was somewhat amused and happy. He seemed to be quite confident of an easy victory over this hated enemy.

The Neanderthal kept his knife low and ready as he slowly shuffled across the open area that separated the two men.

Warily Atia backed slowly away, watching for his chance to do some damage to his over-confident enemy. Atia expected his large opponent to be slow and stiff in his movements but was completely surprised at the extreme quickness that the Neanderthal was showing.

This was the first time that Atia had encountered such an enemy up close and so very personal.

The Neanderthal turned like a cat and struck out hard with his fist, within which he held a medium-sized rock. His blow caught Atia across the knuckles on his knife hand, and the blade fell from his open fingers.

The big man then leapt at Atia, whose response to the giant coming at him was quite instinctive for a man defending himself from a direct frontal attack. Atia struck out with his fists in a left-and-right series of punches to the big man's face. The enemy, however, easily shook off the punches.

Blood was now splattered on the Neanderthal's grinning face, but he completely ignored it and quickly wrapped Atia up within his giant arms in a bear-hug of sorts.

"Now," he grunted, "I break your back, little man." His strength was enormous.

He had seemed huge and fat to Atia's eye, and he was all of that, but he also was a man of unbelievable strength. Those mighty arms that fully encircled Atia slowly began to crush him. Desperately, Atia hooked short smashing blows to his enemy's face. Each of the blows crushed and split the skin of the Neanderthal, but he was quite oblivious to Atia's punches.

The big man slowly tightened his grasp, and Atia felt a streak of agony go through him. He struggled and fought to break the deadly hold, but he could not free himself. Atia felt the breath slowly going out of his body. The monster was leaning his huge weight on him now.

The Neanderthal's mouth was wide and toothless as blood trickled from his lips where they had been split from Atia's blows to his face.

In complete desperation Atia thrust a thumb into his big opponent's cheek and dug his fingers into his enemy's protruding jaw line.

With all of his remaining strength, he ripped at the big man's cheek until something tore beneath his hand.

The giant let out a terrible scream of pain and threw Atia away from him.

It was only a matter of a few seconds until Atia whipped out the second knife that he always kept tied down to his left leg, and with a leap he plunged the needle-sharp blade directly into the giant's hulking chest.

Atia felt himself fainting. Unless he had killed the Neanderthal with that last stabbing thrust, he knew that he, himself, was a dead man.

T IIIᛏ ᛁ̈ᛏ

A bruised and battered Atia woke up from his faint.

It was at that moment that he made a very wise decision that would guide him for the rest of his life.

He realized that it was time to end his private wanderings as a lone hunter. It was time to join one of the local wandering human clans, because they would give him a great deal of security in their numbers. There was always safety in a crowd of people.

A very tired but happy Atia stood up, stretched his aching body, and walked off toward what he thought would be the good life that was waiting for him.

# CHAPTER FIVE

Mog, a Neanderthal, watched quietly from his hiding place as the towering, shaggy, brown sides of the giant bison rumbled along before him.

From where he and his hunting Neanderthal companions lay hidden, they could see the bison's huge humps heaving up and down like the bodies of porpoises soaring from wave to wave.

The bison, with their dark brown-black foreheads, massive dripping black snouts and blood-red eyes, were moving so swiftly that they were almost a blur as they swept by the patient hunters.

Mog realized that he was absolutely deaf in both ears for the moment, and that he could hear nothing but a loud rumbling noise as if the earth itself were seemingly splitting open all around him. These animals were so powerful that he expected to see the ground open up beneath their hooves and fire and smoke to spurt out.

Mog could easily smell the stink of them as thousands of the bison monsters, with their razor-sharp horns, rushed on their way to nowhere.

The bison were sweating with panic due to the heart-stopping labor of their flight across the flatlands of Central Europe.

Mog was not consciously aware of just how he did it but, whenever he did something special like this bison hunt, his physical movements were not controlled by his mind. His actions were governed by his fantastic physical conditioning that allowed him to do things that might have seemed impossible to others. He found himself running swiftly alongside the ever flowing and thundering herd of bison to his left. The flanks of the herd swelled up before him as he turned toward the swarming bodies.

He had absolutely no conscious thought of any danger to himself while the six-foot shoulder-high bison continued running as if time itself were behind them threatening to make them extinct if they did not keep themselves on the move.

Mog and his fellow hunting Neanderthals were so completely intent on bringing down several of the lumbering beasts that they did not pay attention to the large pack of smaller-sized humans who were moving in on them from the surrounding hills.

Mog, who was now running at full speed, gave a savage yell and leaped upward, his powerful hands grabbing hold of the hair on top of one of the moving mountains of flesh.

His foot struck a massive shoulder, and he grabbed a larger handful of thick black fur as he kicked himself upward. As he moved up, he slipped and fell forward. He suddenly found himself lying on his stomach on the back of a huge, lumbering bull.

After losing his hold on the tuft of hair, he grabbed another batch to his right and slowly managed to work himself around so that his legs straddled the back of the beast. The hump on the animal was in front of him and he hung on to it for dear life.

Mog plunged his sharp knife into the rib area of the massive animal, hoping to hit the heart. Before the mount beneath him had time to stumble, he brought his strong legs up so that he was now squatting on top of the spine of the great bison.

He kept his feet together, one hand clenching the bison's neck, as he turned slowly and managed to balance himself despite the up-and-down jarring movement of the great animal.

With a loud laugh and a great smile upon his ugly face, he

launched himself outward and onto the back of the next bison that was running shoulder to shoulder with the animal he had just left.

Suddenly, and without warning, something straight and dark flew directly over his right shoulder. It struck the hump of a bison nearby and vibrated back and forth.

It was an arrow directed at him from one of the human hunters who was running alongside the moving herd.

Mog, one of the rare deep-thinking Neanderthals, instantly realized that both his tribe and the local humans were competing at the same time, right here and now, for the meat that these bison would provide for their people.

The bison, wandering into the immediate hunting area that the humans and Neanderthal tribes both loosely claimed as their own, were not an everyday happening.

Mog was angry with himself for not thinking ahead and realizing that the local humans would be out in full force to kill some of the bison, just as his own people were. Mog was mad at himself for not planning ahead of his immediate needs.

He promised himself that he would do much better in the future—that is, if he had a future.

These humans, who were shooting arrows at him, were extremely accurate with their weapons.

It was a definite fact of life that these two different types of men could not live and work together. It was instant war whenever Neanderthals and humans met.

The problem, Mog knew, was that there always seemed to be more and more of the humans and less and less of his own kind.

Mog instinctively pulled himself up again, this time more swiftly than he had before, so as to avoid having an arrow shot into his exposed back. He jumped from bison to bison away from the outside line of human bowmen and deeper into_ the safety provided for him by the sheer large number of bison that was pounding along beside the animal he was now riding.

One of his feet slipped as he left the back of his last mount, but he was so close to another beast inside that pounding circle that he was able to easily grab hold of another great tuft of bison hair. He just hung there, keeping as low as he could, away from the arrows that were flying everywhere above him.

He touched ground with his feet whenever the huge animal slowed down in its running motion, but his strong arms allowed him to hang on easily, in relative safety.

Finally, after what he thought was more than enough time for the moving herd to outrun the humans, Mog allowed himself to slide down a little, and he pushed himself upward against the ground as he swung himself forward. He got one powerful leg over the back of the animal and came up into a sitting position once again.

A few stray arrows shot at him by the humans continued to fly all around him, but Mog knew that he was well out of their shooting range.

He was busy congratulating himself on his successful escape when a well-placed arrow struck the eye of the bison he was riding. As the animal stumbled forward into the dirt, Mog found himself flying through the air, only to land in an awkward position.

Again, without thinking, he threw himself to one side just as a long spear thunked into the ground where he had been only moments before.

He scrambled to his feet and whirled around to see a lone human hunter advancing toward him with an already-drawn arrow in his bow, ready to shoot.

Mog realized that the humans had outthought him once more. They had probably placed their men all around the outskirts of the valley floor in case something like this happened. Once again the hated humans were much better prepared for the unexpected than he was.

Mog had spent literally thousands of hours practicing his knife throwing. He had cast knives of many kinds at many distances, from all sorts of angles—even while he was standing on his head. He had forced himself to engage in severe discipline: he had thrown the knives until he began to think he was breathing knives and the sight of one made him lose his appetite.

Now the unending hours of practice were about to pay off.

Mog only had time for one throw before the human's arrow that was now being aimed at him was let go. Mog knew that he had to make the most of the split second of time that he had left to him.

His thrown knife went straight and true right into the unprotected throat of the smaller human, who immediately fell like a bag of stones.

Mog quickly ran over to the fallen man and stripped him of all of his weapons. He was especially pleased with the bow and the quiver full of arrows. They were much better made than anything with which he was familiar.

Possibly when he got back to his tribe, he could talk the elders into having some better bows and arrows made now that he had good samples to give them. By giving them these samples, they would easily be able to copy them, and the result would be better weapons for his people. He also took the time to go back and pick up the well-balanced spear that had been thrown at him. He wanted to get a good look at the spear, which seemed to be much more advanced than anything he was used to.

He then had another thought, and it was so powerful that it would change his whole life. Maybe these "better weapons" were something that he should keep to himself so that he could personally look into the opportunity that they might give him.

If he just gave them to the elders, they would take all the credit for themselves. This is what they always did. If this happened, then he, Mog, would have nothing to show for all the danger he had experienced getting the bow and arrows and the better-designed spear. But if he were the one to show the tribe how to hold their own against the humans and possibly defeat them at the deadly game of war, wouldn't that lift his personal standing as a new and upcoming leader for all Neanderthals?

The possibilities that were now flowing through his mind seemed endless, and he was getting very excited.

What if he could put together a group of loyal followers to help him show off the new weapons and to act as his officers in some sort of army? Now wouldn't that be interesting?

With these exciting new ideas rushing around in his active mind, he knew that the first thing to do was to get away from this area where arrows were still flying about and take himself to a safer place.

Without looking back, Mog began a slow running pace toward the distant mountains where he knew he could hide out and be safe while he thought about what he should do next.

He hugged his new weapons to his chest as he began to run at a slow but steady pace.

# CHAPTER SIX

Mog got to the nearby foothills of the Alps just as the sun was starting to go down behind the tall mountain range. He crawled into a shallow cave with an opening about eight feet off the ground.

The first thing that he did was to build a small fire by the entrance of the cave to keep out any wandering animals. Then from his holding pouch, he took out some slices of bison meat he had cut earlier from one of the dead bison lying about. Together with some wild berries that he had gathered, he had himself a very fine meal.

He then wrapped himself in his furs and fell asleep within the safety of the quiet cave. But he did not sleep well. He slept just above the sleep of complete unconsciousness. He dreamed much and also found himself wide awake at least a dozen times. His heart was pounding, and he had trouble getting himself to calm down. Nevertheless, he did sleep better than he thought he would.

The sun was quartering the dark sky before he was fully awake.

He had a quick breakfast on leftover bison steak and sat quietly thinking about how to achieve his grand ideas and the great schemes that were still running around inside his head. They were the very same ones that came to him over and over again. He saw himself as the new leader of his small tribe, and with the new weapons that he would bring to the group, he knew that this was possible.

He pictured his small tribe spreading out from their narrow valley's living space as he gathered many of the other tribes together and made them all into a great Neanderthal nation with himself as the grand leader.

He smiled to himself as he imagined his fighters easily overwhelming the puny humans with weapons that were the equal or better than anything that they had. Mog continued smiling to himself. Dreams were nice but making them work was another thing.

Mog, of course, did not realize it, but he was an exception to the average Neanderthal. He was a deep-thinking man who was able to learn from his mistakes and go on to bigger and better things with the knowledge he had acquired.

He did realize, however, that with a proper plan and new and better weapons, he could tum the whole world around, and if nothing else, he was absolutely determined to try.

# CHAPTER SEVEN

Several months have now passed, and we find Mog in a minor leadership position within his tribe. He is still determined to improve his weapons by any means possible.

"Mog, how are you? It is very nice to see you." This was said by Zak, the very best weapon maker in the entire area.

This greeting was the closest that Zak would ever come to showing enthusiasm for anything not connected to the art of war. Zak's facial expression, however, remained as impassive as it always was.

Zak was a dwarf Neanderthal with thick hair and a bushy beard that was almost completely white. He looked almost as wide as he was tall. His torso and limbs were rippling with muscles.

Despite the cold season he was stripped down to his waist wearing only shorts and sandals. He was covered in sweat and had just stepped outside of his workshop to cool himself down.

Zak was known far and wide as the best weapon maker of all the tribes.

Beyond the doorway against which Zak stood, Mog glimpsed an incandescent glow and could feel the searing waves of heat blasting from the furnace.

Zak's weapons and arms foundry stood almost alone at the far end of the tribal village. The forge was still in the process of being built, but Zak had promised he would start making all the weapons that Mog wanted very soon.

Mog was saying, "Listen to me well, Zak. First of all I want a special sword for myself. This sword has to be so strong that when it strikes another blade, it will shatter that blade completely. This sword must make me unbeatable in a fair fight, and Zak, if you will do as I ask, I promise you that as I rise in fame and power so will you.

"So tell me, Zak, can you make me this sword or do I need to find myself a new weapon maker?"

With a big smile on his ugly face, Zak said slowly, "This special sword is what you want and need. Is that completely correct, Mog?"

"A great sword is what I must have, Zak."

"Do not worry, friend Mog. Zak only makes great swords. Everything Zak makes is always the best. I will make you the best of the best."

"Zak knows everything about swords," the dwarf continued, "Zak knows what nobody else knows, and what Zak does not know, nobody else knows either."

"That is fine, Zak. You will be well rewarded." Mog turned and started to walk away.

"Yes, Zak will make you this fine sword, but first you have to show Zak that you know how to use it.

"Lodnar," Zak shouted up to another dwarf on the roof of the armory. "Bring down two swords."

"What?" Mog cried out. "I'm going to have to prove myself to you before you will make my sword?"

"Aye, Mog. I know that you are our new leader, but you still have to show me that you are worthy of a sword made by Zak."

Although Mog felt annoyed with Zak, he was also quite amused by the idea of having to prove himself to the master swordsmith. It did show him that the arms maker had high standards, and this was most impressive to Mog.

Mog watched as the young dwarf, Lodnar, climbed down the ladder. When he reached the ground, he headed inside the building where Mog assumed the better weapons were being kept.

He noted that Lodnar was much slimmer than Zak and that his short beard was dark red.

Half a minute later Lodnar returned holding two swords, which he gave to Zak, who then presented one to Mog.

It was an excellent sword that Zak handed to Mog. It was well balanced, properly weighted, with good keen edges that were parallel almost to the tip, and which were as sharp as the cutting edge. The handle was bound with very soft leather.

Mog went through a few swift moves with the blade. This was much more for Zak's watchful eye than to test the sword.

The weapon that Mog was holding in his hand would have made him happy if he owned it and could use it in a battle. He was tempted to ask for its price, in that there seemed no good reason to have a sword specially made when this one was more than suitable for his immediate needs.

"Very fancy." commented Zak once Mog had completed his imaginary duel. "You move like a warrior and, from your body scars, I can see that you must have been in a few battles.

But how well can you fight one on one? Let us try a few sword passes together."

Mog raised his sword in his right hand. "You aren't worried that I might kill you, Zak?"

"You kill Zak, and Zak cannot make you a special sword."

"Yes, Zak, that is correct, but if I do kill you, does that mean that I would have been a good enough swordsman for you to make me a blade if you were still alive?"

Zak laughed and suddenly, without warning, thrust his sword at Mog's belly. If Mog had not blocked the blade and turned it aside, he would have had six inches of metal in his gut.

Zak could have pulled back the stroke before striking, but Mog wondered if he would have done so. He knew that he would never know the answer to that one.

They fought, and Mog held nothing back. He knew that he was up against an expert swordsman, and so he gave it everything he had.

To complicate the matter even more, Mog was finding it difficult fighting an opponent whose sword came up at him from a completely different and much lower level than an opponent who would have been close to the same height as Mog. Zak was definitely an expert swordsman, which was extremely rare for a dwarf. Axes were their usual choice of weapons. Zak's technique was not very stylish, and he tended to swing his blade as if it were, indeed, an axe, but his anticipation and reflexes were extremely fast.

To unnerve the dwarf Mog suddenly switched his sword to his left hand and continued with the smooth flow of the fight.

Mog bluffed a move to the left, then drew his sword arm back suddenly as Zak's sword followed his move. Zak was moving quickly to stop what he thought would be Mog's next stroke but, instead of the expected move, Mog suddenly sprang forward with his blade outstretched and still in his left hand.

He leaned back a moment later, and there were red lines of blood upon Zak's chest. There were two intersecting lines of blood marking where his heart lay inside his massive chest.

Zak stepped back and he gazed down at his own blood which now mingled with his sweating flesh. He lowered his sword and bowed deeply from the waist.

"Zak will be honored to make the great sword for his honored new leader," said a smiling chief weapon maker.

That is how the famous sword of Mog became a reality in the world of the Neanderthals.

# CHAPTER EIGHT

Somewhere in the European flatlands. The timeline is still about 5,300 years ago, (which is the beginning of the Bronze Age for modern man).

Five years have gone by and Atia, now a young adult of twenty-two, finally has decided what he wants to do with his life.

For days on end Atia had followed the trail of the Goat Clan as it marched across the rough landscape of the flatlands at the foot of the towering Alps.

He very much wanted this special clan to accept him, but clans rarely had anything to do with anyone outside of their own closely-knit group of traveling humans.

It was especially difficult for a single male like him to be adopted into a group like this, since he was completely unknown to them. This was a fact of his life that he wanted to change.

He no longer wanted to be an outsider, someone whom the families within the clan feared and avoided completely.

Atia had a perfectly good reason for wanting to join this group who called themselves the Goat Clan. It was all because of the woman who went by the name of Ava.

Ava was the gray-eyed one whose beauty could not be hidden even by the ever-present layers of dirt, grime, and obvious ignorance.

Atia just knew that she was the special one whom he had to have as his own mate and so, earlier in the week, he had withdrawn from his own tribe that was also wandering about from place to place in the wide-open flatlands.

He began to trail after the Goat Clan and watch their every move from a distance.

He was sure that they never saw him spying upon them as he followed them while they wandered around to the same general locations.

He desperately wanted the beautiful Ava to accept him. He wanted her to love him as he already loved her.

He finally came up with a plan that he was sure would work. He continued to trail them from afar until he felt completely comfortable that he knew all of their habits individually and as a group.

He was interested in watching the male hunters from the clan as they roamed farther and farther away from the campsite, looking for bigger game and generally finding none.

He took special interest in watching Ava and the other women as they spent much of their day beating the bushes for rabbits, squirrels and anything else nearby and edible.

By sunset they would all gather around their fires, the women cooking their meager meals and the men chipping new tools and weapons from the small stockpile of materials that they each carried around with them in small leather bags.

They were a self-contained, self-sufficient group, living off the land and staying just above the starvation level as long as they did not produce too many children.

The smoke from their small fires did not damage the purity of the air, and their scattered refuse piles did not contaminate the soil.

Their pitiful little camp did not harm the water table, nor did their hunting endanger any animal species.

ꓔ �Ⲓꓲ�<sup></sup> ꓠꓔ

The newly learned wasteful attitude of these simple nomadic hunters would become the ingrained attitude of all the generations of humans that followed them.

ꓔ ꓲⲒꓲ ꓠꓔ

In order to impress the Goat Clan with his great skills as a hunter, Atia began hunting for fresh meat from the game animals in the far-off hills and leaving their carcasses next to the smoldering campfires while the humans slept.

Innocents that they were, they posted no guards as they slept out in the open with just the stars looking down on them.

Their surrounding fires protected them from dangerous night-stalking beasts, and Atia assumed that human tribes other than his own must have been too far away to pose a threat to them.

It was very easy for him to leave them a quantity of rabbits and a small deer or two that he had flushed out of the bush and killed by throwing small rocks at them or by using his bow and arrows.

He watched the tribe each morning from a safe distance, always from concealment behind rocks or bushes.

The people within the clan were startled at first as they wondered how the dead game suddenly appeared at the campfires each morning.

They discussed it for hours at a time, and some members of the clan said that they believed some of their own clan members were doing the good deed and were too shy to take the credit.

But no one admitted to it, and after a few more mornings of finding the gifts by their campfires, they began to realize that it was the work of someone from outside the clan.

The unknown factor of the gifts from outsiders made them fearful, but it did not stop them from cooking and enjoying the feast as if they had caught the animals themselves.

However, they did start to post sentries throughout the night hours just to be on the safe side.

At first they posted sleepy youths, and Atia easily managed to slip past them as he continued to leave them his gifts of many different animals.

Then a few of the adult males stood guard, but it was a very rare night when they stayed alert enough to prevent him from leaving a gift near one of the smoldering campfires.

Gradually, he let them see him but always at a distance. He would hold up a dead goose in his upraised hand or carry a young deer across his shoulders and leave it for them to come out and drag it back to their camp. They would all huddle together and stare at him in awe.

In the dark of night, he would sneak in close to their crackling fire and listen to their talk and, before morning light streaked the sky, he would leave them another prize before he melted away into the darkness.

He listened also to the names they called themselves, and he learned that the red-headed leader was Dal and a teenager with a crackling voice was called Kralo.

He already knew that the woman he loved was Ava, and he found out that she was Dal the leader's woman.

This knowledge hurt him deeply but only for a few moments. He found himself thinking that if Dal were no longer alive, then Ava could no longer be his woman. His heart soared at the possibilities that ran through his mind with these new ideas.

With even greater enthusiasm, he wandered even farther off into the distant hills until he came upon a majestic stag dipping his antlered head to drink from a little pond.

Unsheathing his bow, Atia slowly walked toward the stag. It saw him coming, but it was not used to seeing humans, and that allowed Atia to get within easy shooting range of the magnificent animal.

He felled it with a single arrow through its neck and had no remorse over killing it. He then slit its throat swiftly and cleanly with his knife.

With a determined shake of his head, Atia lifted the carcass onto his strong shoulders and headed back toward the Goat Clan's camp.

The stag was heavy, and he walked slowly and carefully through the low hills that lay before him.

Just as the sky was beginning to darken and the first of the nighttime stars began to show themselves in the sky, Atia stepped into the flickering light of the clan's camp with the stag lying across his shoulders.

The clan was still eating, actually stuffing themselves, as only people accustomed to long hunger will do. Their fingers and faces were greasy with meat, while the campfire blazed hotly in front of them.

Atia stepped into their midst and dropped the stag with a heavy "thunk" at Dal's feet. No one spoke a word. For several moments, the only sound was the hissing of spitted meat burning on the open fire.

"It is I, Atia," he said. "I bring you another of my many gifts."

# CHAPTER NINE

H is beautiful Ava recovered her wits before any of the others, as Atia dropped off his gift of meat at their feet. Rising slowly, she extended both of her arms toward him in a friendly manner.

"We thank you, mighty Atia. What can we do to show you our gratitude?"

Atia smiled gratefully at Ava, while inside his head he was thinking, *there she is covered with dirt and her face and hands are stained with the blood from the red meat she was eating, but here in the firelight I can see her gray eyes shining, and I have fallen in love with her.*

*I don't care about anything else,* he thought, *I just want to be with her.*

Atia took a slow calming breath and tried to speak in the somber manner they would all expect from a visiting great warrior.

He heard himself saying, "I grow weary of being alone. I wish to stay among you all for a while."

That sent a murmur through the clan as Dal got to his feet and stood silently for a moment beside Ava.

Dal asked him, "Why are you really alone and by yourself? Is this of your own choosing? Tell us true, Atia, why have you really come to us?"

With a most charming smile on his face, Atia replied, "My clan, which is called the Clan of the Bear, is far away, and I have been away from them for a long time. I have been traveling on my own adventures exploring the wonderful world that is all around us."

"I have come here to show you some of the things that I have learned about hunting and trapping and how to protect yourselves from your enemies. I have come to you in peace and friendship."

"I have been alone for more days than any of you can count, and I am weary of being by myself. You are the special type of clan that I have been looking for. You are the special people that I wish to make my people."

"I wish to spend my time with you, and I hope that you will allow me to stay." Even as he spoke the words, Atia realized that there was a great deal of truth in what he had said.

He had usually been around friends and family, but he wanted to have a special woman of his own. Hopefully, this was the right time for him to change all that.

Ava, with surprising warmth and understanding in her voice toward this complete stranger, held everyone's attention as she said in a strong and clear voice, "We all know that even the mightiest hunter needs a clan and a family to come back to. We must all try to understand what Atia is really telling us."

Like all humans facing a difficult decision, they finally settled on a compromise. The leader, Dal, spoke earnestly with the two elders of the clan, then with all the adults. They finally agreed to let Atia join them and show them his tricks for hunting. They all agreed that another strong male warrior was a good thing for the clan to have.

The only other stipulation they made was that he had to sleep by himself away from the immediate campsite. This was to be for only a little while until he got used to the members of the clan and they got to know him a little better.

These people did not think much about their future. They only lived in the present moment, and Atia understood all that.

The clan only dimly realized that tomorrow might be different from yesterday, but that was their everyday thought process.

Atia was quite content with their decision for the time being since it brought him closer to his Ava. That was more than enough for him, right then.

T IIⱶ ꝀT

It was that night that she came to him.

Even in the darkness with only the light coming to him from the distant campfires, he could see and smell the blood and entrails smeared on her.

Ava said, "You could not come to me, Atia, so I have brought myself to you."

Part of Atia was disgusted by her and her very primitive ways; part of him was repelled at the thought of taking her into his arms and wallowing in her stench and passion. He knew that Dal would never forgive him for making love with his woman.

But with a suddenness that completely overwhelmed every other thought in his mind, he felt a primitive male lust come over him, and he became as wild and fierce as she was.

For this small amount of time, at least, he would not be alone. He would have his Ava with him.

T IIⱶ ꝀT

Their tongues met, hot and wet and seeking. They kissed for long breathless minutes as they dragged air into their lungs and kissed again.

Atia eased himself more fully over Ava as he intimately rubbed his hard body against her soft curves.

"I don't want to hurt you," he murmured thickly against her lips.

"You won't, I promise you," she whispered as her body was screaming inside for him to touch her. His reluctance was the only thing hurting her at that moment.

"Tell me what you want," Atia coaxed her gruffly. Ava pushed his head down to her full breasts.

As he undid each loosely tied knot, the animal-skin covering on her body fell away, and his warrior's hands shook more and more.

Finally, as the last knot was undone and her wrap was completely unfastened, he shoved the wrap aside and gazed at the loveliness of her breasts.

With a hoarse moan, he dipped his head and took one taut nipple into his eager mouth while his fingers sought out the other. She had barely touched him and yet he felt himself ready to explode.

They moaned in unison when the tight curls on his chest tangled with her taut nipples.

He kissed, licked, and suckled each nipple with a single-minded concentration that soon had Ava moaning and writhing beneath him.

Her fingers clutched in his hair as he continued to lavish his attention upon her well-developed breasts.

"Atia," She whispered in a tortured breath.

"You are beautiful," he ground out roughly. He lifted his head long enough to share another feverish kiss and then his hands and eyes roved farther down her body.

"I want to see all of you, Ava." Atia's eyes sought permission while his fingers continued to roam freely.

Ava lifted her hips up a bit in her answer to his unspoken question. When she was totally exposed to the chilly night air and to the intense gaze from Atia, a tremor coursed over her.

She felt more vulnerable than she'd ever felt with Dal, who was the only man she had ever made love to. She was feeling herself getting far more aroused than she had ever imagined possible.

She began to think that, perhaps, this perfect male, who was causing feelings within her she never knew existed, was the right mate for her. Could he be the one she had been looking for all of her adult life but had never found?

Atia laid a hand on her inner thigh, felt her soft supple flesh and thought that he could hear his own blood pounding in his head.

No female had ever excited him as much as Ava. No woman had ever brought him so close to losing control during his lovemaking as she had.

"Kiss me," she begged hoarsely once again.

That next kiss was hotter and more feverish than all the others.

Their arms and legs entwined while their tongues dueled passionately. Atia thrust his tongue in and out of her mouth as a prelude to the mating of their bodies.

The hot, aching heaviness in his groin intensified until Atia thought that he would shatter into a million pieces. He withstood a few glorious torturous minutes of her many caresses.

A big smile crossed Atia's face as his fingers slipped up her leg to the juncture of her thighs.

Ava gasped at his touch then moaned in pleasure as he gently stoked her most sensitive flesh.

"You're so hot and soft," he praised her in a thick tone of voice. "I want to feel all of you just as you are." Ava moaned and arched her hips against his hand.

The sounds, smells and feel of her arousal sent a violent tremor quaking over Atia's body. The only way that he could contain his own raging desire was to concentrate on something else besides the woman in his arms.

His mouth again found one of her turgid nipples, and this time he sucked roughly, greedily as Ava stifled a scream while the tension in her body began mounting to staggering heights.

Her nails dug into his shoulders as his caresses drove her to a fevered pitch of need.

"Please, please take me now," she begged as her body writhed beneath him.

Atia spoke not a word as he wrapped his arms around her and lifted her gently while positioning himself between her thighs.

A moan got trapped in her throat as she felt Atia's hard, smooth flesh penetrating her body.

Nothing in her past experiences had prepared her for such intimacy.

She was very tense, but his skillful caresses and soft -speaking voice helped her to relax. Then, with only a brief flash of pain, Ava felt his body lock tightly within her.

Atia's body was soaked with sweat. He was fighting off the strong urge for completion of the sex act.

He forced himself to remain perfectly still until Ava could adjust herself to the feel of him inside her.

They clung to each other, their bodies trembling with tension, their eyes locked each upon the other.

Neither of them had enough energy to speak as their bodies began to dance in the age-old rhythm of lovemaking. The sounds they made were private, primitive and pleasing.

Ava sobbed as her body found a release from the incredible pressures within her. Atia watched her with gleaming eyes, and held her tightly until she quieted down.

Once again, Atia entered her, and they soared together to the heavens once more.

The physical effects washed over them like an incoming tidal wave of emotions that took them to the stars.

He collapsed in her arms, and they both fought for breath. When he finally had the strength, he suddenly rolled onto his back and pulled Ava on top of him.

His strong arms encircled her and held her possessively. Atia had never known such overwhelming satisfaction. It wasn't just the great sex, it was having this amazing woman in his arms. Ava made everything special for him. She was sunshine, sweetness and spice.

She made him feel whole and complete, and he just loved it. He liked the way he felt when she was in his arms.

He liked feeling the way he felt right at that moment.

Ava put her hands on both sides of his head. She lifted herself high enough to look him in the eyes. Her smile was adoring. Without another word, she gave him another big smile, gathered up her things and was gone.

Atia just lay back and was fast asleep in moments. He knew that he would be having very pleasant dreams that night.

# CHAPTER TEN

The next morning, the entire clan resumed their trek northward. Each person staggered under a heavy load of dead game that had been accumulated.

Atia was aware that they all traveled under clouds of flies and the smell of decaying meat as they walked along in the warmth of the day. It was enough to make him feel sick. No one else seemed to mind it at all, so he tried to ignore it and kept walking.

All those people around him seemed happy as they each carried their share of the clan's belongings.

Ava walked up at the head of the little column beside Dal. If Dal knew what had happened the night before, he gave no sign of it. Ava gave Atia no sign, either, that their relationship had changed at all.

Later that day, Ava did drop back to walk beside Atia. "Soon we'll be in our special valley," she said.

"Special valley? What makes this one valley different and special from all the others?"

Ava smiled. She looked as pleased as any traveler who was making her way home after being away for a very long time.

"Our valley is a wonderful place. Everyone is happy there. It is always good when the clan goes back there every spring."

When they finally reached it nearly a week later, Atia saw that it was truly a lovely, sheltered location.

They all stood quietly by the bank of a gently meandering stream of water that afternoon just looking across the flat valley below.

The stream of water dropped down a series of terraced stone steps on its way to the floor of the valley before it made its slow way past it and disappeared into the very far-off cliffs at the other end.

It truly was a beautiful location—a paradise of sorts. Atia noted that the cliffs in the distance actually formed the base of a big double-peaked mountain. Far up at the top snow still lay glittering white under the springtime sun.

He could see why the clan was so happy to be here. The valley was sunny and green, and it lifted up any onlooker's spirits just by looking at it.

From its U-shaped cross section, Atia could tell that it had been ground out by a glacier, probably from the looming mountain crumbling away in the distance.

It seemed very secure, quite snug, and easily defendable against any outside invaders if the clan would post a lookout, which, it seemed, they had never bothered to do up to this point in time. ·

The attitude of the clan was, why bother with lookouts when nothing has ever happened here?

The only access to the valley was down the stone-terraced steps of the waterfall area which they were now entering.

It was a really beautiful area, and Atia saw why Ava was so excited to get back here.

The trail was slippery, but not terribly difficult to get down, and on the far side the valley walls rose fairly steeply to heights of at least several hundred feet.

The next few weeks were spent here quite peacefully enough.

Three more very friendly clans filtered into the valley, bringing the totals up to one hundred and nine adults, with dozens of children ranging from nursing babies to gawky preadolescents.

In Neolithic society, where life was short, teenagers became adults as soon as they reached sexual maturity and twelve-year-old females bore children. Forty-year-old adults were often too feeble to hunt or eat, and they were "tenderly slain" by their loving family and clan members.

Ava told him that they always stayed in the valley until the grain that they had learned to plant turned golden in color. Then they would harvest it and carry it with them for the cold winter months.

Every few years, whenever they would have an early snowstorm, all the crops would be destroyed and when that happened, all the clans suffered greatly from a lack of food. This had happened to them the previous year, and that was why they were all so eager to get back to the valley and start planting their new crops.

This was a crucial point in human history. These clans, these dirty, ragged, wandering bands of humans, were going to make the first transition from hunting for food to farming.

They were initiating the Neolithic revolution, creating the most important step that would turn humankind from nomadic savages into civilized city-builders.

Mankind, as a result of agricultural farming, would be on the path toward mastery of our continent. No longer would there be a few scattered half-starved tribes of nomadic hunters, but settled, prosperous farmers with a steeply growing population.

Would agricultural farming be invented here in this valley where Dal and his allies spent their summers? If not this clan, would some other clan or tribe of humans somewhere else in the world take firm hold of agriculture? If so, there would be no holding back the human race from absolute greatness.

# CHAPTER ELEVEN

The grain grew taller than Atia's knees, and the people of all the gathered tribes grew more excited and impatient to harvest it with each passing day.

It was that night that terror struck the quiet little valley in the form of blood-curdling screams that shattered the quiet. Flames were seen to be burning everywhere.

Everyone jumped every which way. A spear thudded into the ground near Atia's foot.

Screaming and yelling erupted as human men and women toppled with large spears driven through their bodies.

The bonfires hissed as blood spattered onto them.

The clans' people ran for their huts terrified, but not Dal.

"They're burning the grain," he was shouting. "Get your weapons. We have to fight for our lives."

Through the flickering flames Atia could see, quite clearly, naked Neanderthal warriors painted in hideous colors dashing into and out of the huts. Some held burning torches and others held deadly pointed spears.

"Demons!" some of the humans screamed, and their call was echoed throughout the camp. They did look like demons and very much nonhuman-like due to the way that their huge and ugly bodies were brightly painted red and black. The firelight sparkled off of their glistering bodies and added to the illusion.

Atia knew that if only Dal had listened to him and had posted a lookout as he had suggested, then all of this could have been avoided. The lookout would have seen the Neanderthals coming and then the clans would have had time to put their defenses together.

Atia calmly looked around to see if he could locate Dal. He watched him as he pulled a spear from the body of a fallen clansman and then began running toward one of the enemy warriors. Ava dashed in behind him, scooping up a fallen spear and advanced to stand with Dal.

All of this had happened within seconds. Atia rushed into his own hut, where he had to knock down an enemy Neanderthal who tried to stop him as he reached for his bow and a quiver full of arrows. The Neanderthal was dead in less than a second.

There was a great deal of screaming and crying over the loud noise of the battle going on all around him.

Atia darted back into the night air outside his hut, sidestepping to avoid a painted Neanderthal who sprang at him with his spear leveled at Atia's chest. Atia floored the warrior with a lethal punch to his neck and stepped over his unmoving body.

Atia stepped out into the flame-filled screaming fury of the battle with every one of his senses alert and sharpened to its finest pitch. He felt a wild exhilaration. The dullness that his life had become was now over, and the battle going on around him was waiting for him to join. His spirits soared with the fight that he was about to enter.

He knew that he lived to fight the good fight, and this would be one of them.

He notched an arrow and sent it through an enemy warrior's skull.

Dal and Ava were off to his right using their spears to fend off four spear-wielding Neanderthals. Atia killed one of them with a quickly shot arrow just as Dal ripped another's belly open.

Ava dropped to one knee as a Neanderthal charged at her. She easily handled him and moved on.

Atia was, once again, very impressed with his Ava. She was quite the female warrior as well as the love of his life.

In the light of the blazing field of grain, Atia could see many of the clans' people on the ground, but there were many more of them on their feet fighting against their mortal enemy.

The invading Neanderthals were beginning to fall back, throwing their torches at the humans to slow down any pursuit.

Sheer maddening anger and the lust for battle drove Atia forward. He raced after the retreating enemy, bellowing mindlessly as he fired his remaining arrows into them. He then took a spear from a fallen warrior and charged at the Neanderthals with all the fury that had been pent up inside him just waiting for this release.

He easily knocked down with a sidelong swipe of the spear the first Neanderthal to take a stand against him. Another enemy loomed at his side, and Atia drove the spear point into his stomach.

He screamed as he yanked the spear free and slashed it across the face of another one.

It seemed a lot longer, but within seconds his spear was bloodied along its entire length and quite slippery in his grasp. He slaughtered anyone who came within his reach.

The remaining Neanderthal warriors bolted, wide-eyed with new-found fear, while he raced after them killing, killing again and again as he caught up with the slower-moving enemy.

Behind him he could hear the shouts of Dal and the others growing fainter.

He followed the few retreating warriors toward the distant cave-dotted cliffs. One of the Neanderthals stumbled and fell in front of him. He drove his spear through him and felt it bite into his body.

The remaining invaders scattered in all directions, their weapons thrown away as they ran for their lives to escape his bloody rage.

He slowed down and turned to look back. He saw that Dal and all the others had turned their attention to the fires that the invaders had started in the grain fields.

He was just able to make out the tiny figure of Ava, smeared with the blood of her enemies, standing triumphantly and waving both arms over her head urging him to come back to her.

Atia ignored all of the distractions and pressed onward toward those caves in the distance from where he knew the invaders had come.

When he finally got to the base of the cliff, it was getting dark. Not even the glow from the burning fields cast much light in there.

But in that hushed gloom, where even the insects and beasts of the night lay silenced and frightened by the rush of fighting men, he heard breathing and the soft tread of bare feet on the stone ground. He moved forward into the caves as if he were unaware of their presence.

The instant they leaped at him, he whirled around and swung his spear at their legs like a scythe cutting the three of them down.

As they fell in a jumbled heap, Atia hefted the bloody spear in his right hand and threw it at the nearest of the two Neanderthals who were trying to circle behind him.

The solid *thunk* of the spear hitting the Neanderthal's chest was louder than the desperate little gasp he gave out as he died.

Atia was able to kill the second warrior with a quick throw of his knife, but the third and last enemy was already running down the ever-darkening tunnel.

The cave that Atia was now entering was even darker inside than the last cave, with not a single glowing ember from outside lighting its yawning blackness. As dark as it was, Atia plunged into it anyway, still hot with his reckless fury.

It was the cave bear's warning growl that saved Atia's life. If the beast had been as intent on killing as Atia was, it would have waited until Atia had blundered into its grasp and then crushed him with its mighty paws. But it was only an animal defending its lair, and it had none of the malicious hatred that human beings carry within them.

The cave bear was a massive animal that lived in Europe and often sought shelter within deep caves throughout the Alpine mountains. The males often grew to as large as nine hundred pounds, which is about three times the size of the brown bears of future years.

Atia was quite familiar with this type of cave bear. It grew extremely large, along with the wooly mammoth, wooly rhinoceros and cave lion.

The animal that he was facing in the darkness growled once before it slashed out at him with a deadly paw. Atia lunged forward with all three of the spears that he had bundled together in his firm grip toward the sound that the bear was making.

Atia was very lucky. He hit the bear's heart or lungs with the wild thrust. One of the spears snapped in his hands, but the other two penetrated and the animal died with a hideous shriek of agony.

Suddenly the bloodlust cooled completely within Atia. He was dripping with sweat, covered with blood from head to toe, and trembling with physical exertion and emotional exhaustion.

Killing other men, either human or Neanderthal, meant very little to Atia but the killing of this innocent animal snapped him out of his battle fury.

There in the utter darkness of the beast's cave, he bent over and fell to his knees, panting and weeping with shame and regret over what he had just done to an innocent animal.

# CHAPTER TWELVE

For several minutes following the killing of the cave bear, Atia remained in perfect silence.

Gradually his strength returned and with it his resolve to finish what he had started.

He wrestled one of the spears from the bear's still -warm body and stepped carefully over the large carcass. He then tried to grope his way out of the ever-deepening darkness of the damp cave.

His eyes were absolutely useless in that black cavern but all of his other senses were back on full alert, and he stretched them out as far as they could reach.

He knew that he had at least one more dangerous Neanderthal enemy still ahead of him.

But just as he could see nothing, he also could hear nothing—not a sound except for his own ragged breathing. The mostly inaudible sound was of his own bare feet on the flat cave floor. His left hand slid carefully along the rough stone wall, and in his right hand, he held the last of the deadly spears. He advanced very cautiously, probing the darkness like a blind man, seeking an enemy that he knew was lurking out there somewhere ahead of him.

As he stepped further into the wide cave tunnel; a tremendous blow to his head caused him to fall forward into an open pit lying ahead of him completely unseen.

Atia felt himself passing out into unconsciousness.

𒀭 𒐁 𒀭𒋾

When he finally opened his eyes, he was feeling the very chill of death upon himself. The lump on the back of his head was huge, and it was throbbing. It was all he could do to ignore it.

He looked around and saw that he had fallen downward into a pit about twenty feet deep. The huge open ceiling through which he had fallen was high above him, and he knew that it was completely out of his reach. Fortunately, though, there was a gaping hole in one of the side walls and enough light was coming through for him to see fairly well.

He could see his breath puffing from his open mouth. He was beginning to shiver involuntarily. He sat up very slowly and propped his back against an outcropping of ice.

His head was thundering from the blow that he had just received, but with a conscious effort, he worked at easing the tension in his neck muscles.

He assumed that the last Neanderthal, who had sent him plunging into this open pit, had fled the caves above him.

He was no longer fighting a mortal enemy but simply the cruel and completely uncaring elements of nature, which he knew could be the most terrible enemy of all.

In the complete and absolute silence that surrounded him, he was able to hear the sound of trickling water. As he got up and started to move around, he soon realized that the rocks were getting warmer, and that the ice was slowly beginning to melt.

The heat that he was now beginning to feel seemed to be coming from a natural source somewhere below him. Magma, volcanic liquid rock, from a large underground volcano was rapidly heating up the whole area. He could see the bright red glow coming through the icy ground beneath him.

Now the answers to the many questions that had been bothering him for the past few months became clear. The reason that the clan's special valley was so green and lush when everything else was very dry and lifeless became understandable and quite obvious to him. The minerals and underground warmth provided by this volcanic heating system kept everything growing and warm over the many years that Ava's people had been coming here.

Atia continued to hear a very loud slapping noise from the area far below him. Waves of water seemed to be surging through the underground caves.

He realized it was the large amount of ice that was rapidly being heated and melted by the awakening volcano that was forming this sudden growing body of water.

"A flood," he said aloud, his strong voice sounding strangely hoarse and muffled against the close walls of the rocky chamber in which he seemed to be trapped.

Atia's thoughts were suddenly racing, and none of them were good. He reviewed what he thought was happening hoping that he was wrong and that he was missing something.

He knew that the underground heat that was melting the glacial ice would definitely cause a large accumulation of water. The water would then turn into a flood, and that huge amount of water would pour into the entire lower valley and all the people within it.

The most important thought of all was the fact that Ava, his Ava, was right there in the danger zone with all the rest of the combined clans.

It was a disaster just waiting to happen unless he could do something to turn things around.

Even as he stood there, it was slowly beginning to happen.

The water was noisily lapping deeply below from where he was standing. It was rising and getting closer and closer with each passing moment.

He had to escape from this underground prison.

He had to get down to his Ava to warn her and the rest of the clans that they had to get out of the valley and find higher ground, and they had to do it right now.

He took a deep breath and rolled over to the edge of the very steep drop leading down toward the rising water.

There was actually no time for him to feel any fear as he plunged downward.

He oriented his rapidly falling body with his feet downward, which he thought was the best way to take such a huge drop.

If he dove into the water headfirst, the speed and impact when he hit the water might knock him out and then he would be helpless.

He did have a moment to wonder just how deep the water was really going to be.

He just might smash his body on the rocky bottom before he drowned. Anything was possible.

The water felt like a solid sheet of rock when he finally hit it, and then he was plummeting deep down into the icy black water, where every nerve in his body was shocked numb. There was no sensory awareness except for a painful bubbling in his ears.

He bobbed to the surface at last, took a deep breath and half swam, half rode the current to wherever it was taking him.

Atia had the distinct feeling that the swirling water was taking him in the opposite direction to the one where he had originally entered when he met the cave bear. This meant that he was being rushed away and being taken farther and farther from the valley that he needed to get to.

After what seemed like hours, he banged his head against solid rock while the river continued to swirl and surge all around him, pulling him this way and that.

He was feeling a strong current that pulled him along until finally it dropped him into another tunnel longer and deeper than the one he was in. The water just kept pulling him along at its own very rapid pace.

He knew that he had no choice as he realized that fighting against the water flow was useless, and so he filled his lungs with great gulps of air and dove under the water in the same direction that the current was taking him.

He just wanted to cut down on the time it was taking him to get to wherever it was that he was going.

# CHAPTER THIRTEEN

It seemed like days until the darkness around him began to brighten up, and he was suddenly thrown to the surface of the raging water.

Air, real fresh breathable air. It tasted wonderful as his barely surviving body returned to life. He felt himself gulping in huge amounts of the most precious substance on earth—plain, breathable air.

The river was now emptying itself into a huge cave, turning it into a vast underground storage center.

He dragged himself up onto dry rocky ground, every part of his body jangling from lack of blood circulation.

From far overhead sunlight was actually filtering in at him from an opening in the huge cave. He knew that he was much too weak to eyen try to reach it.

For hours, there was nothing he could do but lie there on the rock-strewn dirt and try to recover his strength.

But with every moment of his recovery time, the water behind and below him rose higher and higher, splashing and gurgling as it filled this natural underground storage cistern.

Soon enough the water began lapping at his feet as he lay stretched out, prone on the wet ground.

He forced himself to stand up, and he began to climb the sloping wall of the gigantic cave. He was trying to work his way toward the opening that was just below the high ceiling where the sun's light was streaming in.

The bare earth was loose and pebbly and was very difficult to climb. With each step forward that he took, he was in danger of sliding all the way back down again to the waiting waters. But he continued to struggle upward and finally was able to push himself through the narrow fissure of rock and out into the daylight sun.

Looking down, he saw that the underground river was still rapidly filling up the cave. When it finally reached the rock ceiling that he had just crawled out of, the water would have nowhere else to go but outward. When that happened, it would explode through the rock wall that was holding it back. With massive strength, it would burst outward and then down into the valley below with the force of a tidal wave that would easily sweep away everything that stood before it.

Atia staggered down the steep slope of the low mountain and headed for the distant valley. His legs were weak and rubbery from all of his recent exertion.

Through blurring eyes, he could see the valley spread out below him in the late afternoon sun. It was beautiful, peaceful, and extremely vulnerable to the forces of nature that would soon be heading its way.

Atia knew that he had to get down to Ava and Dal before the water swept them away. He had to warn them and all the other people who were still in the valley trying to put their lives back together after the Neanderthal attack.

Even as he walked, the mountain began to grumble, making the very earth itself tremble. Hot steam was beginning to boil up from the volcano's cone, and Atia knew that worse things would soon follow.

The gentle stream that used to meander slowly through the center of the valley was now rushing and roaring, already starting to overflow its banks.

It was beginning to edge into the grain field as it burbled the full length of the flatland and splashed into the lake that was now growing at the base of the waterfall.

The formerly gentle waterfall was now a much angrier one. It had become very powerful as it poured an even stronger torrent of water down the stone terraces and into the waiting lake below.

Mist rose from the lake and caught the slanting rays of the dying afternoon sun in a diabolically enticing rainbow.

Even though Atia was still a great distance away, he could see that most of the valley had fallen into shadow.

The stream was still spreading its growing fingers in all directions as it rapidly flooded the entire grain field and edged toward the huts that the clans had built.

The waterfall at the far end of the valley was lost to his sight due to a heavy mist that had formed in front of it. He could actually hear its thundering roar even from that distance.

The volcano's rumblings grew stronger and angrier as it began to spout black smoke streaked with red flames.

As Atia stood there watching with a horrified feeling in his heart, he saw a wall of white water blast down toward the valley, roaring like all the demons of hell had been let loose at the same moment.

Steam hissed into the dark sky, and a hot rain began to fall all around the valley floor.

Atia found himself running as quickly as he could down the slanted mountain. He wanted to get to the people and somehow save them, but he was much too late.

He could see quite clearly the drama playing itself out ahead of him. He could see the people standing there frozen in terror as that all-consuming wall of water hurtled toward them.

He turned to look through the darkness as the flood surged below him. It frothed and lapped at him as if it were angry that he had escaped from its grasp by being on higher ground.

Within minutes the crest of the floodwaters had passed him by.

All that he could now see ahead of him was a great nothingness where the little village used to be.

Everything and everyone had been washed away with the rushing water, never to return.

As he stood there at the edge of what used to be the village center, he felt as if he were the only living thing for as far as the eye could see.

With a heavy heart, he turned southward to once again rejoin his original clan. He had found that he enjoyed the company of other human beings, and he needed to seek them out. He would never forget Ava and Dal and all the rest of his newly made friends. But life was still strong within him and he felt great hope for his own future even without his beloved Ava.

He slowly took a last look around when suddenly a large object shot up to the surface.

With a great smile on his face, Atia recognized just what it was that he was looking at. He dove as quickly as he could into the now absolutely calm water and swam out to the object floating just ahead of him.

There, clinging to ropes that Atia had tied together for his huge wooden tribute to the gods of war, was the woman who held his heart. It was Ava who had the presence of mind to rush into his hut and secure herself to the only thing that she knew was large enough to support her weight and protect her from the waters that she saw rushing down toward her.

T IIГ ҒГГ

Hours later Ava is seen trudging through the muddy terrain about ten yards ahead of the slowly moving Atia. She stops, turns and comes toward him. He opens his arms in a comforting gesture, and she slowly flows into them as he tenderly embraces her once again.

T IIIꜰ ꜰT

Ava had been thinking to herself that Atia would be able to protect and provide for her. He was wise, strong, and she knew that he wanted her. He would be a good provider and she would be his mate. Maybe the gods that had saved them would bless them with many sons.

They stood there quietly for a few moments just looking into each other's eyes. The future was out there for them, and they would face it together.

# CHAPTER FOURTEEN

**M**og was *very* excited.

He had just been invited to appear before the elders' war council for a second time. It was this council that controlled most of the Neanderthal warriors who loosely made up the fighting strength of the four largest Neanderthal tribes.

It had not gone well when he had made an appearance before them several weeks ago. He had ended the meeting by telling them that they were old and foolish men who would not change their old -fashioned ways of doing things.

He told them that they had to adjust to the changes that were going on in the real world and if they could not do that, then they should get out of the business of war.

He also told them that the humans with their better bows and arrows were keeping them, the Neanderthals, away from the good watering places and away from the animal hunts that were needed to keep their people alive.

Mog took the elders outside of their campsite and showed them how the bows and arrows of the humans could easily outshoot the farthest hand-thrown spear.

Τ ΙΙͰ ͰͳΤ

He said that he wanted their authorization to produce a great amount of these bows and arrows, and then train the Neanderthal warriors in how to use them. He said that in order to get their warriors on an even footing with the humans, the bows and arrows and the latest weapon, called a sword, were absolutely necessary.

His arguments fell on deaf ears. The council concluded that since time began the Neanderthals had fought with spears and knives, and they would continue to do so.

Mog stormed out of that meeting and went back to his clan, where he was accepted as their leader.

He still had Zak, his weapon maker, working on the bows and arrows and swords. Then yesterday he had received a message asking him to kindly report to the council's next meeting three days off. The message also said that Snark would be at this meeting and to please be ready to answer General Snark's questions.

Mog had never met Snark, the military leader, but he had heard all about him, and from what he had heard, it was not a good thing to meet up with him.

It was said that Snark had killed more Neanderthal warriors in hand-to-hand fighting than anyone else before him. Snark had moved up the ladder in the army's leadership by challenging each Neanderthal leader who was above him.

In personal combats to the death, it was said that Snark had defeated each senior leader one by one. After his fifth straight victory, there was no one ahead of him anymore, and by default he became the Supreme Leader. However, during the past four years under Snark's rule, things had not gone very well. The humans were taking over practically everywhere. It seemed that there were just too many of them, and it was becoming very difficult to keep track of their movements.

It was whispered quietly that the council would like to get rid of General Snark, but there was no one to step into a leadership position as long as he was alive. Based on these thoughts and rumors, the clever-thinking Mog was able to put the clues together and come up with what he thought was the reason the elders suddenly invited him back to their next meeting.

They probably liked his suggestion of upgrading the army's weapons, but they knew that General Snark would try to keep things the way they were with no changes. Mog thought that they invited him to their meeting with the hope that he would challenge the general. If he could defeat him, they would get rid of Snark, and, at the same time, get the new weapons that Mog was talking about getting. If things went well, it could be a win-win situation for them.

The days until the meeting had passed very quickly, and Mog was finishing up his speech before the council and Supreme Leader Snark. "… and I have come up with a plan to use the humans' new weapons against them.

I plan to use brain power, not just muscle, to rid ourselves of the threat they present to all of us.

Thank you for allowing me to make this information available to the council and to you, Leader Snark."

The room remained silent for a few moments until Snark stood up, and all eyes turned to him.

"Members of the council and Warrior Mog, I wish to share a few thoughts with you."

"I have been hearing from my spies that the war council would like to learn more about these new weapons our friend Mog has been talking about. I am always interested in learning about new things, so here are my orders. Kindly listen carefully because I expect all of you to act exactly according to my wishes."

"In two days from now at the open fields behind the campgrounds, I will have my best spear thrower show what a spear can do."

"I expect Mog to show up with his new bow and arrows. If my man wins the contest, then there will be no more discussion of which weapon we shall continue to use to fight. If my man loses, bows and arrows will be added to our fighting equipment."

"I notice by the nodding of the council members' heads that this first of my three points is acceptable and approved."

"My second point is that Mog will present himself in a sword-fighting contest with one of my men who has been practicing with this new weapon. If Mog loses, there will be no more discussion about swords. If Mog wins, then swords will be added to our daily weapons."

"And my third and final point is directed at you personally, Mog. I sense in you a challenge to my authority, and I hereby challenge you to a wrestling match to the death. Most of our warriors will be present to watch one of us emerge as Supreme Leader."

"If you defeat me, and I caution you that I have never lost a match, then you will have the senior war-leader position. If I defeat you, you will be dead, so it won't matter to you.

"I take it by the nod of your head that you accept my challenge. I'll have one of my staff make all the necessary arrangements and advise you of the time and place.

"Thank you, all."

With a big smile on his ugly face, the Supreme Leader left the meeting room.

All was silent as each man in the room was thinking about what had just been said and what would be happening as a result.

# CHAPTER FIFTEEN

I t is now the morning of the next day after the meeting with the elders and leader Snark.

Mog had slept a peaceful night and had just finished his breakfast. His body was rested and his mind was whirling with good thoughts. Everything had gone his way yesterday, and he had gotten everything that he wanted.

Not only would he be able to introduce the new bow-and-arrow weapon, but he would also introduce the sword as an official armament for the warrior army that he planned to put together.

Everything was moving along well.

All he had to do was defeat their best spear thrower, fight their best swordsman, and finally kill Leader Snark. It should prove to be a most interesting day for him.

He felt confident that he could dominate all three areas and, if this proved to be true, then the world was his for the taking.

A big smile crossed his face as he thought about what he should do right now to take his mind off of tomorrow.

What he needed to do was to relax, and the best way to do that was not to think about his big day tomorrow. It would come soon enough.

The best relaxation for him always was to take a female

Neanderthal or female human to bed.

This time it should not be just any of the ordinary girls who hung around the camp waiting on his pleasure. This time he would take the new female human captive that he had ordered held by herself in a special hut. He had posted a special guard at the entrance so that no one else could get at her until he was through with her. He liked to always be first with new slave girls.

This human female had struck him as being different from all the other captives that passed through the camp on their way to becoming slaves to the Neanderthal families. This one had caught his eye. She was tall for a human and she was rather slim, but what had caught his attention were her great breasts.

Mog like all males, whether human or Neanderthal, had a weakness for female breasts. It just seemed to be a part of the male's sex drive and this female definitely was different.

Breasts among female Neanderthals came in all sizes and shapes, and most were rather boring. Human females usually were the complete opposite of female Neanderthals in that they were extremely flat chested and had little if anything to catch the eye of the males.

This one, whose name was Kat, was the exception to all the rules when it came to female human breasts. This one was definitely full sized, well-shaped, firm and uplifted.

The truth of the matter was that from the time Mog had first looked at the batch of newly captured female human slaves, he had felt his palms get sweaty and his breathing had become heavy.

He knew that he badly wanted to grab onto that great-looking chest and all the other female parts that came with it.

He had just been so busy lately that he had put her under guard until he had the time for her. Now was that time.

He looked at the report on Kat, which was made by the elder who inspected all the new captives, and found out that she had never slept with a male before this. It had stated that she was a virgin at the ripe age of sixteen which was very unusual. It seemed that she was a complete innocent when it came to making love, and this also was attractive to Mog in a female.

He sent one of his guards who had been posted outside his own hut to tell Kat's guard to deliver her to him within the hour. He told the guard to make sure that she was properly washed, and that she would be wearing some suitable clothes. Mog always thought that it was fun taking off the female garments.

Before Kat was delivered to him, he wanted to inspect his bow and arrows and to check on his new sword to make sure that everything was in perfect order for tomorrow's competition. He needed everything to be ready to go.

This would be the first chance he had to break in the new sword that he had had Zak make for him.

It was important that the sword taste blood before he took it out on the battlefield.

Ͳ ΙΙΓ ͰͲ

Time passed quickly, and at the end of the hour the tent flaps were opened and Kat stepped in. She was looking good to Mog. Her hair, which when he last saw her was hanging down and was rather stringy, was now piled up on top of her head in a bun. It was tied up with a thin strap of leather wrapped around it.

Her eyes, which were normally a blue-gray color, had a light-colored powder of some sort around them that made them look even larger than they really were. She had a matching color of rustic red on her cheeks and a touch of it on her lips.

It was obvious to Mog that she had taken the time to make herself look attractive to him, and he thought that she had succeeded. He liked what he was looking at.

It was clear that she had taken a bath. Her pale skin was glowing, and the one-piece coverall that she was wearing showed off her legs to good effect.

But for him the best part of what she did to herself was to wrap herself up in a tight-fitting leather wraparound that pushed up her wonderful breasts and gave him just a little peek at the mounds of pleasure that her well-padded bundle promised him.

All in all she appeared to be one well-put-together female human, and Mog really appreciated the time and effort that she had taken to make herself look so good.

Her face lit up with a smile as she looked at him. Mog was not sure if she smiled because she liked him, or because she was just being smart and knew that if she pleased him, her life as a slave would be made much easier.

Mog was thinking that a good-looking human female would not be a bad thing to come home to after fighting in the wars all day.

Kat was obviously quite aggressive as she walked over to the nearest of the two chairs that stood off to one side of the large room.

The rest of the room was made up of Mog's super -large bed and table.

As she sat down, she very carefully and properly crossed her legs and looked up at him.

"Mog," she said. "I saw how you looked at me when you saw me for the first time. I saw the look on your face, and I knew that look meant that you wanted me."

"Obviously, here I am, and you do have me but it is not as simple as that. I know that I belong to you, but that is only my body."

"If you treat me well and honor me as an equal bed-partner, I will not only give myself to you and to you alone, but I will do so with great excitement, love and something else that is very special and something that only I can offer you."

"I can give you my intelligence, which I have been told is very high. I can explain to you how the humans plan their attacks and what surprises they could spring on you. I can make your life so much easier than it must be now."

She looked around at the simple room and Mog, who was following her eyes as she looked around the room. He actually felt somewhat taken aback at how simple his room must look to her.

She continued speaking. "You see, my father was high up on the human council, and I was allowed to sit in and listen to their planning discussions. I know how the human military mind works. You be good to me, and I will be good to you, Mog."

She stopped talking and looked up at him, and then added, "You must know by now that I have never been to bed with a man, neither human nor Neanderthal.

So, if you show me what it is that pleasures you, I will be trained by you, and I will know what you like to do in bed.

"I only ask that you be gentle with me this first time since everything is new and scary to me right now.

Please don't hurt me."

Mog said not a word and walked over to where she was sitting. Extending his hand to her, he helped her to rise out of her chair.

As easily as he would scoop up a baby, he lifted her and carried her gently over to his bed where he deposited her down in the very center. He placed a large pillow under her head and looked down at her.

He liked what she said, and, besides being the best-looking female he had ever seen, she was smart and knew many things that could be very helpful to him with his planning.

He promised himself that he would be very gentle and kind to this human female slave named Kat.

# CHAPTER SIXTEEN

Looking down at her, Mog undid the ties that were holding her wrap together. He had to pause and catch his breath once again as he saw her fully for the first time. She was like a white-colored panther, all female, with rippling young flesh, and not a single trace of fat.

It was surprising to have found a fully mature sixteen-year-old woman who was still a virgin. He tried to remember what it was like to be sixteen years old. He felt old at twenty-five. He felt old in the way that trees and stones and mighty civilizations feel.

Whenever Kat moved around, trying to find a comfortable place on his bed with pillows under her head, it was only her full breasts that moved about, and once again, they were Mog's focal point.

He lay down next to her, and they looked at each other. Both of them were surprised at what they saw in each other's face.

When she snatched a shaky breath, and inhaled the masculine scent of him, a strange heat collected deep within her. Butterflies rioted in her stomach as her eyelashes fluttered up to meet those fathomless pools within his eyes. Kat felt as if she were being absorbed into the depths of those spellbinding eyes, as if her energy were flowing into Mog like a swift current following the channel of a river. When his full lips descended upon hers in the slightest whisper of a kiss, Kat felt herself melting.

He was without a doubt the most perfect male Neanderthal specimen upon which she had ever cast her eyes. This warrior was a living column of imposing strength, possessing well-proportioned shoulders and a chest like solid rock.

His muscular body carefully glided over hers before he quickly slid onto his side and off her. Kat felt a wild, uncontrollable tremor flooding through every nerve in her body as a wave of panic accompanied those soul -shattering sensations.

Before Kat lost her composure, Mog backed away, as if he knew by instinct that he dared too much too quickly with one so inexperienced in the intimacies between male and female. Kat swallowed hard, trying to ignore the many tingling sensations that spilled through her body.

She very nearly leaped out of her skin when Mog touched the peaks of her breasts and lifted a questioning brow. His eyes twinkled, but no smile touched his lips. Kat felt like she would die of embarrassment at the familiarity of his touch. Her modesty was the price she knew she had to pay to establish a bond between herself and her new master.

Kat found herself gently drawn down onto the animal skin as hard-muscled flesh half covered her and heightened her awareness of this intriguing Neanderthal. He was a paradox of tenderness and omnipotent strength.

She sighed audibly as this male instilled an indescribable longing inside her. His gentleness stripped away her inhibition as if it had never existed.

When his mouth slanted over hers in a tender but possessive kiss, Kat surrendered without a fight.

Mog was teaching her not to fear him, and she responded with an ever-growing sense of trust and a burning desire to investigate the mystical dimensions of pleasurable sensations.

When Mog's hands glided up her thigh, Kat swore that her flesh was about to melt off her bones. His explorations of her body spurred a need that was fast becoming an addiction within her. His caress was so gentle and unhurried that she was helpless to object.

Her mouth opened to the silent demand of his kiss. Their tongues mated, their breaths merged, his hands skimmed over her belly, and Kat felt warm tingles burgeoning inside her.

When his hands scaled the ladder of her ribs to swirl over to her breasts, Kat felt hot desire riveting her naive body. She arched helplessly toward him, granting him privileges he had not even requested. His hands and lips were teaching her startling discoveries about intimacy, and she instinctively responded to them.

What was the matter with her? The way she shamelessly yielded to this Neanderthal's tender touch … one would have thought that she had been a harlot in another lifetime.

Mog lowered his head to brush his lips over the soft pink buds of her breasts, savoring the texture and scent of her skin. His tongue flicked out to tease the rigid peaks, and he felt her luscious young body quiver in response. When he suckled her dusky crest, her body instinctively moved toward his.

His arms glided over her shoulders and she trembled with a need she had never known.

Kat's breath lodged in her throat when his hands and lips feathered over her body, finding and sensitizing every inch of her flesh.

Kat could form no protest as Mog explored her body completely. A flood of embarrassment stained her cheeks while she watched his eyes travel from the top of her head to the tips of her toes.

Sensations spilled through her just as surely as if he had reached out to caress her. Such a potent gaze, such an incredibly tender Neanderthal, she thought to herself.

Part of her was thoroughly ashamed at her lack of feminine reserve, and another part of her defied conscience and restraint, aching to discover where these delicious sensations would lead.

Until this moment Kat had been naively unaware of the powerful undercurrent of desire that could drag a female into its hazy depths and drown her in her own desires.

Over, and over again, languid kisses and caresses flooded over her flesh.

Kat became the center of a pulsating awareness that throbbed in spellbinding rhythm. She gave herself up to the wild, mindboggling sensations that had her swearing she had come to life for the very first time and at that very moment.

She was astonished by the maelstrom of emotions she never knew existed, and she ached for more of these wondrous torments.

A gasp tumbled from her lips when his caresses became far more daring and erotic. He guided her thighs apart with his knees and bent to spread a row of heated kisses over her belly and the complete curve of her hips. When his hands glided lower, Kat completely forgot how to breathe or why she needed to. These remarkable sensations she was experiencing were more than enough to sustain her.

Her body shuddered in uncontrollable spasms when his fingertips began to explore the very essence of her femininity.

He stroked her and aroused her until she convulsed around him, lost in sweet, torturous pleasure. Suddenly his intimate caresses were not enough to satisfy the monstrous ache that swallowed her alive as Kat clutched at him, her nails digging into the scars on his shoulders and back.

When she drew her quivering hand across the velvet male length of him, the breath she had been holding gushed out in a ragged sigh. She was touching him where he was most a man, and it sent her senses reeling, escalating her own pleasure. She dared the inconceivable and yet it still did not satisfy this white -hot need that coursed through her.

When Mog showed her how to please him with her untutored

caresses, she gave no thought to right or wrong; only to the compelling power of her passion in its purest, most unselfish form.

Kat reveled at this new-found power she suddenly held over this magnificent giant Neanderthal. For all his brute strength, he had become her slave, moving on her command.

It was as if he had suddenly begun to live through her touch to his most personal of male parts, and touch him on his manhood she did.

She gave him caresses and kisses that expressed her own need to return the pleasure he had bestowed upon her in his bed.

She wanted him to know how he had affected her. She carefully watched him succumb to her now-bold caresses on his man-tool as completely as she had succumbed to his touch moments ago.

Mog suddenly rolled over and got above her while she still held the pulsating length of him in her hand. He ached to feel more than just the throbbing need of his desire surrounded by her fingertips.

He wanted to become a part of her for one great and glorious moment that would capture time itself for them both.

His mighty arms trembled as he held this little wisp of a girl, refusing to frighten her and yet aching to devour her.

Kat flinched when she felt the penetrating full length of him searing into her like velvet fire. Pain suddenly shattered the spell that she was under, and she instinctively began to push him away.

"NO! PLEASE STOP!"

Mog had depleted every single ounce of self-restraint that he possessed. He could feel passion spurring him on like a merciless rider. This, Mog decided, was the worst kind of torture that a man could possibly endure. He could not hold himself in check a moment longer.

His need had become so dominant that it crippled both his mind and body. He would make this lovely siren forget the initial pain when he swept her up with him to heights that overshadowed the lofty peaks of the mountains.

Kat swore her body had split asunder when Mog thrust himself deeply into her tender flesh.

She suddenly could not draw a breath, nor could she move on her own. The pain intensified as he glided upon her with a steady rocking motion that pressed her deeper and deeper into the bed.

A hoarse cry tumbled from her lips, but Mog smothered it with his possessive kisses, sharing his breath when she could take none of her own.

And then the most paradoxical sensation claimed her. It was an exquisite pleasure born of pain.

Kat could feel her body accepting him, like a new blossom unfolding in the warmth of the early morning sun. It was as if her naive body had suddenly acquired instincts that were completely unknown to her.

She began to move in time with him, meeting each hard-penetrating thrust. She was being compelled by some nameless sensation that expanded at a phenomenal rate, like a ball of fire consuming all that was within its path, feeding on its own raging flames.

Kat felt like a meteor blazing across the sky, charting a course to its own destruction.

Sensation after sensation converged upon her until she cried out in the overwhelming wonder of it all.

She swore that she had left a permanent mark on the Neanderthal warrior when another spasm of rapture riveted her. Her nails spiked into the tendons of his arms, her legs curled around him, holding him, arching ever closer to the maddening need that engulfed her.

Every ounce of self-control abandoned her. The hypnotic sensations recoiled upon her, bombarding her at the same breathless moment. Wild spasms raced through every nerve and muscle, and Kat clung to Mog as if he were the only force in a swirling universe. Indeed, at that moment, he was.

She was living and dying in the same fantastic moment.

When his powerful body suddenly shuddered upon her, another wave of sensations crested over her; stripping every last fragment of thought from her mind.

For what seemed forever, Kat lay there, her body intimately joined with his as if she were a living, breathing part of this incredible male force of strength.

A lazy smile pursed her lips as her hand absently trailed across his hips to investigate the corded muscles that lay there.

How very easy, she thought, to fall in love with a Neanderthal man such as this gentle giant.

On those contented thoughts, Kat drifted off to sleep to relive the erotic moments in her dreams.

# CHAPTER SEVENTEEN

Mog, who was normally an early riser, threw a cover over the sleeping human woman and then quietly slipped out of the peaceful hut.

The human female, Kat, had more than pleased him. Not only was she nice to look at, but he knew that with a little more practice, she would be the greatest bed-partner that he had ever known, and he had known them all.

There was something about this human female that touched a soft spot in his heart. It may have been because of the toughness of her fighting spirit. Mog always respected a warrior, whether male or female. Even though Kat knew perfectly well that she was just a slave, she stood up to him and spoke to him as an equal.

She did not hesitate to offer him her body, and then the hint that she could supply him with vital information about how the humans went about the business of war was something she knew would hold his interest. This was one very smart female human.

It was Mog's master plan to unite under his personal command all of the Neanderthal tribes and all of the smaller clans into one well-trained and well -armed fighting force. If this Neanderthal army could be taught to follow orders, then they would be unbeatable. No one would be able to stand up to the Neanderthals' ferociousness and strength. The problem, as he saw it, was that there was a definite lack of cooperation among his people, and this was what caused all the problems that he would have to overcome.

It was the nature of the Neanderthal males to want to go their own way, at their own pace, and in their own time. This did not help in trying to organize them into a trained and formidable fighting force.

The humans, who always appeared to be under one or more centers of control, fought against the Neanderthals anywhere they found them, and they always fought as an organized group.

Whenever the two groups of hunters met, it was the humans who almost always won the day.

Another point that bothered Mog was that if ever a large party of Neanderthals invaded a human camp, they would, of course, kill the human male warriors and take the females captive. But when human hunters came across Neanderthal women, they would kill them right on the spot; therefore, there was no future for his race unless they could wipe out the humans completely from the face of the earth. Since the humans were spreading out and traveling everywhere, it would soon be impossible to stop them.

Another major problem—and this was a big one—was finding enough Neanderthal males who were smart enough to give and receive orders in an organized manner.

Most Neanderthal males that he knew and came in contact with did not seem to have enough intelligence to lead others, and without officers, an army cannot work well.

But this morning as he woke up and looked over at the sleeping human female lying next to him, he had what he called a brilliant idea.

What would happen if he made Kat into a commander and allowed her to find and train other intelligent human captives to create an officers' unit under her control? Rich rewards for the human captives and the promise of a good life with the new army should get their loyalty. Kat was the key to this.

This idea of smart human females organizing and controlling his warriors seemed to fulfill his basic needs.

He started to get excited, as he usually did when he thought of something clever, but he soon calmed himself down. He had a few things that he had to take care of first.

He had to get past General Snark and the weapons events, as well as the wrestling match, before he could allow himself the luxury of thinking about all these other things.

The time for action was upon him, and he was ready to go.

It was now late morning, and the crowd had been gathering for many hours. Their numbers were impressive. There must have been thousands of on looking Neanderthal warriors packed onto the hillsides that looked down at the flat central area of the large training field.

The council of elders had put out the word that several new and highly advanced weapons were going to be introduced. This would be followed up by a spear contest and a bow-and-arrow contest, and finally by a fight to the death between Leader Snark and a challenger to his leadership, Mog, a high-ranking Neanderthal of good standing.

The council was sitting just off to the left of center of the flat archery shooting range, and everyone was watching the workers set up several bullseye targets for the archery contest.

Standing center stage was Mog, who was loving all the attention that he was getting. He was dressed in his finest furs and was talking with several of his household staff.

To the right of Mog and his little group were two Neanderthal warriors who were known as experts in the use of a thrown spear.

The events were just about ready to start, and a hush came over the usually loud Neanderthal crowd.

The shooting contest was going to be divided into two parts.

88

The first part was an event to show the range and accuracy of a regularly thrown spear as it went up against the new bow-and-arrow weapon that was being shown officially for the first time.

Most of the onlookers were quite familiar with the arrow part of the bow and arrow, because it was the arrow, all by itself, that would come flying at them whenever they were involved in a fight against the humans. The bow part, however, was not familiar to them, and this contest would allow them to see how everything worked, and if this weapon was going to be the weapon of the future.

After the welcoming words were given to one and all by the elders, the three men entered the shooting area.

There were two rows of targets set up in front of the area where the contestants were standing. Each target was made up of what was called a bullseye. A bullseye was the circular mark in the center of the target, and it was this circle in the center that the shooters would try to hit.

The targets were five-foot leather-wrapped wooden squares with a small circle in the middle and larger circles around it. The targets stood on wooden bases and were fairly sturdy.

The target in the first row of the contest was set up about fifty paces away. Fifty paces after the first target, there was a second target. After another fifty paces, there was a third one and, finally, a fourth target, which was again fifty paces after that.

Mog and one of the spear-throwers walked over to the shooting area, and each nodded politely to the elders, each other, and then to the crowd, who had all settled down into silent observation by this time.

The spear-thrower took his time and finally selected his first spear from a group of seven.

The spears were all made of smooth wooden shafts with a sharp point of stone at the tip.

Mog moved out of the way as the spear thrower mentally

measured his distance to the first target and let his spear fly. The thrown spear flew straight and true and hit the target just outside of the center bullseye. It was an excellent throw.

With a wave of his hand, the spear-thrower stepped out of the shooting area, and Mog slowly moved in.

Mog had placed seven of his carefully inspected arrows on the ground. He selected one of the arrows and moved to center stage where he made a show of putting the arrow into its place on the bowstring and then pausing for a few moments before he let the arrow go.

There was no wind to interfere with the flight of the arrow as it struck the first target perfectly centered in the bullseye.

His many hours of practice with the bow and arrows were paying off as the elders declared both shots as being excellent but the winner at the first target was Mog.

There was loud cheering in the background from the packed onlookers.

Once the first target with one arrow and one spear sticking out of it was removed from the field, the spear thrower stepped into the throwing area that had been vacated by Mog.

The spear thrower had selected another spear, and with a practiced eye, he let it go. It nicked the outer edge of the bullseye on the second, farther target. It was an outstanding throw.

Mog moved to center stage once again and shortly let fly his second arrow. It also flew straight and true and it hit the very center of the bullseye.

Mog was mumbling to himself one of his favorite sayings, "It pays to practice, practice, practice. After all, practice makes perfect."

Mog was quickly declared the winner, and as the second target was taken away with the spear and arrow still sticking out of it, the hush of the crowd became absolute once again. The competition had reached the point that everyone had come to see.

᛭ ᛁᛁᛁᛀ ᛀᛁ᛭

The next target, which was the third one in the series, was a very difficult and hard-to-hit target because it was one hundred and fifty paces away and was considered the extreme outer edge of where a thrown spear could go. This was the usual distance where the Neanderthal spear-throwing warriors were in danger of having the human arrows shot at them without their being able to return the fire at the humans with their spears. It was a rare Neanderthal who could throw his spear as far as where the third target was.

The second of the spear throwers came to the staging area for the first time. He looked much stronger than the first thrower and had tremendous shoulders and arms.

All eyes were on him as he took aim and then, with a little run to gather momentum, let go with a terrific heave of the spear. The spear went up and flew right toward the target but the distance was just too great. The spear ended up a few paces short of the third target.

All eyes were now on Mog, who was loving every minute.

Almost casually, he selected another arrow from the few that were left, walked slowly up to the staging area, took aim, and let the arrow go. It landed just outside of the center of the target.

A gasp came from the crowd as Mog very quickly walked over, selected another arrow, paused long enough for everyone to get a good look at him, and then let fly an arrow at the fourth and final target which was another fifty paces away, making it a two-hundred-pace target attempt. This was unbelievable.

The arrow landed this time a little off from the bullseye center, but close enough to get the crowd on its feet screaming his name.

It was a clear and absolute victory for bows and arrows or, as Mog later would tell it, an absolute victory for Mog. Mog had made his point and won that part of the day.

He walked around the staging area and waved his arms at his

adoring crowd. He held the bow above his head for everyone to see, and another great cheer rose up and thundered back at them from the surrounding hills.

Now everyone loved him, and he knew it. Everyone had Mog on their minds and Mog on their lips as they all left the archery area and headed over to the area where the new sword-fighting practices were held.

No one in the entire crowd was going to miss this. Even the elders were showing excitement as they walked across the fields to get to their exclusive ringside seats.

# CHAPTER EIGHTEEN

While the huge crowd was leaving the archery area and getting settled into the large bowl-shaped fencing arena, Mog slipped into the tent that was being used for the warriors to prepare for their contests.

As he was about to step out of the tent and back into the outside fresh air, he was pushed back inside by Kat. Her hair was down, and she had a wild look in her eyes.

Mog figured that she must have been watching the archery contest and, from the very look of her, she seemed to be taken up with the excitement of the moment.

She spoke not a word as she pushed Mog into one of the nearby walls. She grabbed his face and kissed him with a passion that reminded him of yesterday's bedtime.

She still had not made a sound as she placed his right hand inside her wrap where he felt her breasts, which were pointing out at him, firm and full.

She was moving his hand all around, and he was thinking that this was a wonderful sensation for him, when suddenly she pulled his hand out of the wrap, kissed him on the cheek and dashed out of the hut on her way to the next event. Mog was still thinking about Kat's touch. He felt pretty good about her being around. He found her to be very exciting.

If he were still alive after all of this, Kat would be a most interesting puzzle for him to solve both romantically and militarily.

Mog had had many women in all of his past years, but none of them ever expressed their feelings for him like this human female. He smiled to himself, took a few deep breaths and put Kat completely out of this mind.

He went over to the watering area, poured water over his head to cool himself down, and laughingly left the tent to head over to get his sword.

He was totally puffed up and ready for the next event.

Mog was surprised to see so many female Neanderthals in this crowd after seeing so few of them at the archery contest. He thought that the possibility of a sword fight, which would draw blood, might have excited the females more than archery.

T IIᴵᴵ ᴵᴵᴵ T

The supreme leader of the elders, known simply as Wolf, had been running things for so many years that he could not remember a time when he was not the head Neanderthal. He even looked old, and that was very unusual for a Neanderthal.

When Neanderthals got to be in their late thirties, and they were unable to hunt or take care of themselves very well, they were usually turned out of the tribe and left to wander in the wilderness until either the cold or a wild animal did them in.

Before Mog entered the arena, he asked the Wolf if he could speak with him privately outside. The two of them walked a little ways away from all of the Neanderthals who were dashing about.

Wolf was an exception to the old-age rule. He was old. No one knew how old he was, but everyone knew how smart he was, and so he was allowed to stay with the clan.

Elder Wolf was the one who originally organized the tribes into different family units. He set up a simple system of Neanderthal helping Neanderthal when it came to food, weapons and slaves.

He was now smiling his ugly smile at Mog and telling him how pleased he was that the bow and arrow would soon be the weapon of choice for every Neanderthal warrior.

He was very understanding when Mog told him that the schedule of archery, sword fighting and the wrestling match to the death were too much for one day.

Mog made the important point that even if he were successful in the upcoming sword fight, he would be too exhausted to stand a chance in a hand-to-hand battle for the military leadership against Leader Snark.

Mog was very sure of getting the leader's cooperation when he made his request, based on the greed for which Wolf was famous. It was always said that if there were a profit to be made, then Wolf was the councilman to go to.

Mog requested three days delay so that he would be at full strength for the wrestling match. His request was granted without further discussion, since Wolf knew that an offer was coming. In return for the delay, if and when he defeated Stark, Mog would double the take that the council was now getting in food, slaves, and weapons. Mog could see the greed lighting up the leader's face as he thought about the offer.

Having sealed the deal immediately with the usual hug and pats on each other's back, Wolf limped his way back into the packed sword arena to take his front-row seat. He said that he would announce the three days delay if Mog were still alive after the upcoming sword match. Mog had to smile as he watched the old Neanderthal walk away. Now all that Mog had to do was survive the upcoming sword fight that was scheduled to begin in a few minutes.

He was very excited to break in his new sword, and he was curious to see which of the three champion swordfighters he would be facing.

If Mog had to pick one of the three to do battle against him, he would pick Killer Xan. Xan had never lost a match. It was said that there were nine kills credited to this fighter. Mog hoped that Xan would not be Stark's choice, but the only way to find out was to get into the arena. With a shrug of his mighty shoulders, Mog headed for the arena that was putting forth a massive amount of noise from the cheering.

# CHAPTER NINETEEN

*Mog was right.*

S tanding right in the center of the raised arena was Killer Xan. Before he stepped into the dueling arena, Mog took a few moments to study his new and very dangerous opponent.

Killer Xan was a female, and a female swordfighter was a rare thing in the land of the Neanderthals. Mog understood that some females were more ferocious than their male counterparts, but this female went beyond the norm for a female swordfighter because she was a female sword-fighting *human*.

Mog remembered the surprise he felt when he heard about Killer Xan's success in the arena against both males and other females. Most of her victories were against male Neanderthals, but there were a few male humans mixed into those numbers.

Mog's last swordfight had been against his weapon maker when his special sword was being made. Since that day, he had performed his daily drill quite faithfully with the weapon and was comfortable with it and with himself as a duelist. He was ready to do battle.

As he looked at Xan, who was just standing there quietly, waiting for her opponent to enter the arena, he saw a tall, slim, flat-chested human female dressed in typical human fighting clothing. She did not look like anything special, but Mog knew that looks did not kill nine opponents without ever getting a scratch from any of the fights. Obviously she would be a deadly opponent who was probably quite ruthless. He had heard that she had quick reactions and was a very deliberate fighter.

She was a pale blonde with light green eyes, and under different circumstances he would have enjoyed knowing this human female.

He noticed that even though she was standing there waiting for him, her tall, slim body seemed poised and relaxed. Her confidence level must be quite high.

Mog stepped into the arena and faced her. She instantly took up a stance with the tip of her sword pointed at his face.

Mog drew his sword. Not a word was spoken between them.

The crowd was quiet as the fighters circled each other.

Mog held back his attack, hoping that she would make the first move and show him something about her fighting style.

Xan feinted and he parried her move easily. She lunged forward again and he parried again as their swords struck each other and rang out.

She was testing his speed and skill level before she got serious about coming after him.

Apparently he had not impressed her very much, as an almost-mocking smile flitted across her pretty face. She was sure of dispatching him quickly and easily.

Her next attack came with blinding speed, sure footwork, and some unconventional sequences of thrusts and counterthrusts.

Her whistling blade probed his every defense as she moved with amazing speed.

Mog could barely cover himself as he quickly retreated backward from her intense forward attack.

*Wow; she was really fast.*

One of the big differences between fighting a duel, which is made up of only two duelists, and fighting on a battlefield, which involves many fighters, is that in a duel it doesn't hurt anything at all to surrender some territory, which Mog was doing. Mog yielded before her onslaught. Her skill with a sword dazzled him. He had never come up against anyone like her before.

This was how a duel was supposed to be fought.

Had Mog been just a happy spectator instead of the target of her complete fury, he would have absolutely marveled at her technique with a sword. Instead it took all of his efforts just to hold her off. Her attacking stamina was incredible.

As the minutes passed, cold sweat began to trickle down his face and back. His heart was thundering in his chest while she barely seemed winded. The worst thing of all was that she never left room for a counterattack. The few openings that he found and probed met with her swift and immediate counter-response.

Again, and again she drove him backward. Whenever he did manage to take the offense for a minute, he unexpectedly found their positions quickly reversed, and she was in control once again.

He switched from right hand to left hand with his sword. She did the same.

Their blades rang as loudly as before when they came together.

She threw him back ten feet as she rushed in with a series of savage downward blows that would have crushed a lesser man's defenses.

This time he blocked her stroke with both of his hands on his sword as he put all of his strength into his swing. If nothing else, he knew that he had her in sheer physical strength.

If only he could break her grip and send her sword flying, the match would then be over.

But somehow, even though his strong counterstrokes must have numbed her arm from fingertip to shoulder, she kept a firm grip on the hilt of her sword, and even managed a backhanded slash that would have laid his chest open if he hadn't leaped back in time.

Panting and glaring at each other, they circled again and again as she switched back to a right-handed grip once more.

Sweat finally began to trickle down her face. Clearly he wasn't the easy target she'd expected.

*Maybe I could use that to my advantage,* Mog thought.

"We could call it a draw," he said aloud in even tones trying to sound reassuring and in complete control.

"Shut up. Just shut up and die," she responded.

She rushed Mog again with her sword swinging back and forth, and once again they came together with a series of nerve-shattering blows.

She carefully launched herself straight into another series of half-crazed moves that forced Mog backward once again.

Thrust. Parry. Thrust.

꓄ ꓲꓲꓵ ꓩꓵ꓄

A duel is different from a battlefield fight in other ways besides the ability to retreat. There is no moving tide of men around the fighter, no war cries, no death screams, no clashing of sword on sword coming from all directions to distract the swordfighter or the opponent. Everything comes down to the quickness of the blade, the steadiness of the arm, and the sureness of the footwork.

If an advantage cannot be gained any other way, the only way left is to try to wear down the opponent.

Unfortunately Mog felt outclassed. Only by the barest whisker of speed did he manage to hold his own. He felt himself weakening, even if he didn't yet show it in his swordplay.

He knew that he would have to end the fight—and soon—before Killer Xan took advantage of a too-slow response from him.

Mog began to time her moves, waiting for his chance. Ignoring her sword and ignoring all logic, he moved up close to her and with the handle of his sword, he punched her in the head.

The blow would have staggered any normal human, but she barely flinched.

He saw that the edge of the sword handle had nicked her forehead. Blood began to run freely down her face and into her right eye.

"Yield," he commanded. "That is first blood, and it should end this duel."

Mog saw the first turndown of her mouth as if she suddenly began to doubt herself. He also noticed that the blood already had begun to affect her vision.

Unfortunately she disengaged and retreated, wiping at her forehead with the back of her hand. That only helped open the bleeding wound farther.

"Yield," Mog said forcefully, as he advanced on her. "Throw down your sword. This doesn't have to end in your death."

"No." She glared at him, the pure hatred in her eyes telling him more clearly than words that she would never give up.

Mog thought that he might also be able to turn that to his advantage. After all, she hadn't been able to touch him yet.

She had to be wondering if he could be the better swordfighter after all.

"You can't fight with that wound," he announced in a light voice, as if he had known all along that he would come out the winner from their duel.

He lowered his blade slightly as if he had nothing more to fear from her. He thought that this move ought to infuriate her even more than anything else.

"I will spare your life if you surrender. I am always generous in victory."

It worked. Her eyes narrowed to slits and her jaw tightened.

"Mere luck," she snarled.

"You're welcome to think so," Mog said, giving her his very best soft laugh, "but this is twice that I've gotten the better of you.

Do we have to make it three times before you give up? I'm trying not to hurt you."

"This fight isn't over yet."

"Yes, it is, and you have lost it. Look at you. Your hands are slick with your own blood and sweat. You can barely see me. Just face the fact that this fight is over for you."

She did not reply, but instead rushed at Mog, shouting her loud battle cry.

He parried her rush and responded to it. This time she was the one who barely leaped back in the nick of time as Mog's blade came awfully close to her.

Still laughing softly, he stalked forward.

Her eyes flickered with uncertainty as she saw the determination coming from Mog's face to the tip of his sword, and she began to retreat.

He had her. He knew it then. Her spirit had been broken.

Though she might fight on, she no longer believed she could win.

"I demand for the last time that you yield to me," Mog cried.

"I NEVER YIELD." She took in a breath of air, then raised her sword and rushed at him.

Giving his full voice to his own battle cry, he leaped forward to engage her.

He used both hands on his sword, parrying her increasingly wild and frantic swings. Then he seized the initiative and hammered at her.

Their swords screamed as they struck each other.

Again, and again, he pounded at her defenses without any hesitation, without any mercy, and without any pause.

Blood and sweat still streamed down Xan's face and into her eyes, half blinding her. She was now barely able to keep Mog's sword at bay. He felt her weakening, and that gave him new strength.

He smashed his blade across hers and with a dull *crack*, her sword completely shattered.

The hilt of the sword tumbled from her suddenly nerveless fingers, and she gasped in pain.

The tip of his blade hovered an inch from her throat, and he once again paused.

"Yield," he commanded. "this is your last chance."

"Never" she cried as she grabbed at her belt and tried to draw a knife.

He tightened his resolve, took the proper stance for a straightforward thrust, and ran his blade through her heart.

He withdrew his bloodied blade, turned completely around, and walked away from her fallen body with a smile on his face.

He was able to do this because, after all, he was a Neanderthal.

# CHAPTER TWENTY

everal hours had passed and a tired but happy Mog was home spending some quiet time with Kat, who had made them a simple dinner.

It wasn't long until Mog's fingers slid carefully around her soft neck as he tenderly kissed her lips with a slow, sexy, lingering kiss. Kat could taste the juice that Mog had had for his last drink at dinner that night as well as taste his obvious desire for her body. Kat sighed deeply and returned his kiss as she wrapped her arms around this great hunk of Neanderthal masculinity.

All the females at the arenas, both human and Neanderthal, were talking only about Mog. He was the biggest and most exciting male to hit the tribal scene for a long, long time.

Kat had listened to all of them talk as she sat quietly, smiling to herself. Everyone could talk all they wanted, but the reality of the matter was that she was the one that Mog wanted.

She knew that it was her job to keep him happy, and she was very excited about the new world of sex that he had opened up for her. She now felt like a mature woman.

What Mog had mentioned to her about training other female humans as officers in the army he wanted to put together from the tribes and clans was interesting. He had asked her if other human females could be found among the slaves who would be smart and aggressive enough to be officers.

He had said that he would make her senior officer, and she would be involved, along with him, in training them. It was very exciting as he went on explaining a little bit more of what her involvement would be.

There was only one person standing in the way of the planning he was outlining, and that was Leader Snark. Mog reminded her that he was scheduled to meet the leader in a challenge match in two more days. The match would take place in the same arena where the sword fight had taken place.

He said that it was going to be a fight to the death, and the winner would take everything that was hanging in the balance. The fight would have to be a fair wrestling match in front of the huge crowd and the ruling elders.

The winner would become the Supreme Military Leader, and the loser would be dead.

If he died, then Kat would be taken away. She would just be another human female slave.

But if he lived, there was no limit to what life would become.

She shortly gave herself completely to him once again. She loved the feel of the hot warmth of his mouth pressing up against hers.

The feel of his rough hands running over her naked back as he held her close seemed so right. It was wonderful having him touch her as she felt the heat of his body coming through to her.

Suddenly they were deeply kissing, drinking in each other with a deep intensity.

Kat felt as if she would simply die if she did not have more of him.

Her tongue stroked his in return. He twined his fingers into her hair, tugging away the leather band holding it at the nape of her neck.

She leaned firmly into him and felt the thick ridge of his erection.

Mog quickly filled his hands with her high, full breasts and stroked her plump pink nipples.

He lifted her up and carried her over to the waiting bed where he deposited her face down. He carefully positioned her so that she was on her hands and knees. He showed her how to lean forward and put her weight on her hands, which gave the rest of her body more freedom of movement. She immediately caught the idea and lifted her rear end up higher with her legs nicely spread apart.

Mog was very pleased that there was little, if any, need to have to talk to this compliant female.

He reached forward and played with her beautiful breasts once again. She really had a great set of breasts.

He slowly entered her from the rear and carefully began to pump into her with a slow but ever-increasing motion. Kat caught on fast and shortly the two of them were pumping away together for all they were worth.

Minutes later, Mog was done, and Kat, with a loud scream, completed her act.

# CHAPTER TWENTY-ONE

It was finally the day of the big match. The weather was cool with just a hint of a chill in the air, and Mog was all ready to go. Today was going to be the most physical of all the contests that he had gone through.

He had said goodbye to his staff and had gotten hugs and kisses from Kat, who had a worried look on her face. Not only was Mog's future going to be determined by the outcome of today's event, but hers also.

After eating a hearty breakfast, Mog walked over to the arena where he and Leader Snark would be competing.

Everything seemed to be in good order. The entire area was surrounded by a special group of warriors who would be standing around the outside of the wrestling area to make sure that no one from the crowd interfered with this most important event.

The area where Leader Snark and Mog would be doing their best to kill each other was out in the open so everyone could see that the match was fair and proper.

Since the winner of the match became the one in charge of the Neanderthal warriors for all the tribes and clans, everything had to be completely open for all to see.

The match was scheduled to begin in about an hour, and Mog

watched the crowd as Neanderthals entered the hills surrounding the arena.

It was interesting to see that there were what seemed to be an equal number of male and female Neanderthals.

It was unusual to see so many females, but the blood sport that this match would be probably caught their attention.

The only female human that Mog saw was Kat, who was sitting in one of the rare chairs next to his new friend Wolf.

He obviously had a good eye for women and would claim her for his own slave girl if Mog came out the loser.

T IIᑊ �T

In every group of fighting males, there is always a bully. It is usually a big shot who, through his size and strength, or through political connections, thinks that he is better than the rest of the fellows.

This surely described Leader Snark, as Mog stood there calmly staring at him. Snark was a big man. Mog sized him up as being at least five foot three, which was tall for this group. He must have weighed close to three hundred pounds.

This great big bully boy looked formidable indeed as he walked around the wrestling area raising his massive arms, thumping his chest with his great fists, and shouting out clearly the names of those whom he had defeated in the last five events. Many of those names were probably quite familiar to the overflowing crowd, because the mention of each name of the former leaders brought forth gasps of appreciation from the massed onlookers.

Leader Snark stooped over in the center of the arena and went into a deep wrestler's squat where he raised first one leg and then the other. He then stamped his feet on the earth for effect as he played to the crowd.

He was working up his energy level as he whipped his arms back and forth across his heavy chest, slapping his own sides with blows strong enough to knock down the average Neanderthal.

A heavy-fleshed smile spread over his ugly face, and his eyes narrowed to even thinner slits as he looked Mog over.

What he saw in Mog was a slimmer-waisted, wider-shouldered and well-muscled Neanderthal who was at least two or three inches taller than he was.

Leader Snark continued to watch Mog as he took his turn to walk around the arena. Snark was making mental notes to himself as to how Mog moved and carried himself.

Unconsciously Mog's hands began to flex into fists as he also began a series of moves to loosen his muscles and warm up his body.

A shiver ran through Mog with the anticipation of the battle that was coming up against this giant of a Neanderthal who was standing there quietly watching him. In spite of the danger of the situation he was now facing, Mog felt that once he got into the match, he would enjoy the extreme physical contact. There was a feeling that lived within him that always answered the call to battle. It was a strong inner emotion that he could never completely control.

Even now the emotions of the crowd washed over him as the adrenaline inside his body began to flow. He felt the veins in his thickly corded neck beating rapidly, and his skin was being stretched taut. He was ready to fight.

Leader Stark continued to stand there quietly as he watched the Neanderthal on the other side of the arena begin to loosen up as he moved about.

Stark over the years had learned many moves similar to the movements that Mog was making. They were very deceptive and possibly quite dangerous.

Snark also noted that there seemed to be absolutely no fear in this Neanderthal as he went through his warm-up drills. He could even see a little smile playing around Mog's lips.

There should have been wariness or at least some caution behind the eyes of this Neanderthal, but Snark could see none. All he could see was a coolness that made a tickle under his own scalp grow into an irritation.

He found that he, Snark, was acquiring the signs he was looking to see in his opponent: fear.

They began to circle each other. Snark's first thought was to simply rush the lighter Neanderthal and overwhelm him, but he quickly discarded the idea.

They continued to circle each other, each looking for a weakness in the other Neanderthal's style, one where an opening could be found.

Snark had been fighting for many years against unthinking opponents, where the fine art of wrestling to the death had never been quite as refined as Mog's skills seemed to be.

Snark had lost none of his wrestling skills over the years as he had gotten older, and he too was ready to do battle right now. He had always relied solely on his superior brute strength plus a few often-tried and well -tested tricks to achieve his many victories.

He was trying hard to concentrate and to plan his attack, but to the surrounding crowd of onlookers it appeared that he was stalling.

Calls of "Shame, Snark!" and "Snark the coward!" came at him from the crowd as he continued to circle around Mog.

To be called a coward by those men, whom he could crush with one blow, was not to be tolerated, as the calls struck at his pride and hit him like so many whips slicing him to his very soul.

Snark's face flushed with shame. Never had this happened to him before.

He knew that he had to bring the fight to Mog, as their circling slowly grew closer and tighter until they were only a few feet apart from each other.

If he could only bring Mog to where he, Snark, could use his greater size and strength, then all would be well.

Snark extended his hands. He splayed out his fingers, offering Mog a choice. To go into a classic beginning wrestler's grip or not was to be Mog's decision. Mog only nodded slightly and extended his own hands in reflection of Snark's move.

Tentatively they reached out their hands, barely touching their fingertips at first. Next the fingers intertwined and locked. This was the first test, and it was a test of pure brute strength.

Snark's face grew taut as the great muscles in his neck and shoulders bunched and tightened, while he ever so gradually began to apply more and more pressure.

Snark let his strength flow down into his arms and then into his hands where they were being gripped by those of Mog.

As Snark's strength came to him, so did some of his lost confidence return. He could feel his power grow as he began to turn the wrists of Mog to the outside.

Once they reached the point where the elbows were locked, Snark knew that it would take no more than a tiny bit of pressure, and Mog's elbows would pop loose from their sockets. Then, at his leisure, he, Snark, could toy with his victim until he decided to end it.

Mog's wrists did turn. They were forced almost back to the critical point and then the movement stopped completely. Snark's efforts were frozen in place. No matter how hard he tried, he could not move Mog's wrists any further.

Snark drew on more power from deep down in his heavy belly. He searched for his body's center and drew more strength from it. He transferred the power that he found there back up to his chest, then down into his shoulders, arms, hands, and, finally, to the very tips of his fingers. But it was to no avail. Mog's wrists would turn no more.

Snark tried to dominate his opponent by locking eyes with him to try to force his strength of will and impose his physical power over him. This was a big mistake.

Snark's own dark eyes found nothing in the eyes of Mog that gave him any comfort. Instead, there was calmness but no peace in those eyes that looked back at him. It was like looking into the quiet that usually preceded death and destruction.

Mog's wrists began to tum, but not outward. They were slowly returning to their original position.

The doubts that Leader Snark had felt earlier now rushed back upon him as he tried to look away from the eyes of the younger Neanderthal.

Snark began to realize that no matter how hard he fought, he had already lost.

But, if he, Snark, had to die, then he would die well, as a warrior should.

For several seconds the two Neanderthals stood locked in time as each of them was drawing upon his own innermost and last reserve of strength. The vertebrae in their spines crackled audibly as the· great muscles surrounding their bodies twisted and contorted.

Their feet dug deeply into the dirt. Their toes searched for a grip as they strained against each other.

The crowd went completely silent as they realized the fight could now end only in a crippling injury or death.

Mog felt Snark begin to give way. The trembling in the giant's arms transmitted signals through their vise-locked fingers.

Tightening his abdomen, Mog sucked in a rasping breath, held half of it, then suddenly relaxed as he twisted his body to the inside of Snark's. At the same time, his feet turned on their toes until his entire body was facing backward inside the extended arms of the giant Neanderthal leader Snark.

His fingers still locked with Snark's, Mog forced their intertwined hands into a crossbar over his head. This was a move that he had been practicing every day since he knew he was going to meet Snark in the arena. It was Mog's superior mind power that allowed him to think ahead, and that gave him the advantage that he had over his fellow Neanderthal.

Mog lowered himself still farther until he was in a deep squat with his buttocks nearly resting on his own heels as the startled Snark went flying over him.

There was no way that Snark could have straghtened out his arms. His own heaviness forced his elbow joints to separate and crack as he hit the ground.

The sound of Snark's landing was like that of a tree branch cracking in the freezing cold of the icy northlands.

Snark's screams covered most of the sound as his body flew through the air to land on his back. His arms were now useless and hanging at his sides.

Mog swung around to rest his legs on top of the fallen Snark's chest. He knew what had to be done if he were going to finish off this affair once and for all.

Reaching down, he grabbed the big man's head with crossed arms, one hand behind Snark's large head and the other on his jaw.

Drawing in another deep breath, Mog screamed as he released the force within his abdomen at the same instant and snapped Snark's neck.

Mog threw back his head and gave his very best victory yell, which caused everyone in the entire arena to jump.

Mog was screaming out his defiance at the world. Mog was here to stay.

# CHAPTER TWENTY-TWO

H is name was Avoti. He was the first-born son of Atia and his mate Ava; following custom, he was named after both of them.

Bronze Age humans believed that if they gave up letters from their own names, the Gods would look down upon their children with great favor.

Ava, by tradition, gave her son two letters from her name and Atia, the proud father, did the same. They added the vowel "o" and came up with the name of Avoti for their first born.

Avoti was born fourteen years after the flood that had wiped out Ava's Goat Clan. He was born into the Bear Clan, which was the clan that Atia and Ava had rejoined after that terrible day.

Avoti, at age thirteen, was already accepted into the clan as a full male hunter.

His father had taught him proper use of his weapons and how to hunt and survive in the unforgiving world into which he was born.

He had already made his first kill of a deer, which provided the clan with enough meat to celebrate his step into manhood.

And now we find Atia and Avoti far away from their usual hunting grounds as they are exploring the distant hills.

Both father and son were intent on following the trail of the wild horse that always seemed to be just ahead of them.

They were heading down a small hill into a flat valley when they suddenly were confronted by two huge Neanderthal males who were following the trail of a different horse from a different direction.

The four of them instantly went for their weapons, which at such a close range meant knives and swords.

Atia's quick mind was the first to realize that he had only a few moments to mount his attack against these historical enemies.

He was quite concerned for the safety of his young son, who had never had a close encounter with Neanderthals and the great danger that they represented.

While the two were somewhat distracted by the chance encounter and before they were able to give their full attention to the two humans, Atia leaped upward and dived upon the nearest Neanderthal's broad back.

His left hand went around the giant's thick neck, trying to tug its heavy head upward so that the dagger he had taken from out of the sheath strapped to his leg could easily slice into that vital area.

But he was unable to lift that monstrous head. Atia's strength was no match for the Goliath that he was riding.

Atia had to change his rushed strategy and simply began to plunge his twelve-inch razor-sharp dagger again and again into the chest and upper body of his antagonist.

The Neanderthal screamed and writhed as its blood fountained.

Atia drove the knife into its tough hide again and again. At each stoke, the creature screeched out its anger and its agony while it twisted and turned until the clinging Atia was finally thrown off.

Atia rolled aside as the enemy staggered upright. One of its hands went to a large gash in its neck as if to try to stop the flow of blood. The blood itself was a sickly red-green color. The brute stared at the wetness on its hands, seeming not to understand what it was. It opened its mouth to bellow out its rage, and more blood trickled from between its canine-like jaws.

The monster's eyes narrowed as it stared at its tormentor, and it lurched toward Atia. Atia felt the fetid odor of its hot breath, and he gagged.

Atia, of course, was much smaller than the Neanderthal, and he was a lot faster. He was able to dodge aside and easily avoid the groping hands that were trying to grapple with him.

He did a calculated flying tumble and

quickly pulled out his sword from the sheath at his waist and yelled out some instructions to Avoti, who was having problems avoiding the grasp of the other Neanderthal.

"Avoti, try to keep the other one away from you by using your sword. He won't want to get close to you if you keep waving it in front of his face!"

Avoti pulled out his own sword and turned to face the second Neanderthal, who had thrown down his spear and pulled out his own very long and very dangerous sword.

Avoti took the on-guard fencing stance that his father had drilled into his head.

He knew that he had very little chance of defeating this huge enemy, but he would try and hold him. off until Atia could get to him.

Meanwhile, Atia stood facing the bleeding predator that loomed far above him, its huge bulk blocking out the dawn sunlight.

Atia felt trapped within the ominous shadow of the monster man. He felt fear, but not for himself. It was fear for his son, who was fighting for his life against tremendous odds.

Atia knew that it was up to him to make sure that the two of them would survive this terrible situation.

The monster was lurching toward him with its mighty arms swinging wildly, but this time, instead of attempting to stay away from those brutal arms. Atia sprang upward to meet the creature head on.

He was holding his dagger in both of his strong human hands as he came down from his leap, and struck deeply at the creature, striving to impale it upon the sharp point of his long blade.

The knife sank deeply into the tough hide of the Neanderthal. It sank up to its full twelve-inch length, and the wounded scream given out by his enemy was more agonizing and fearsome than ever.

The Neanderthal's razor-sharp fingernails clawed frantically at Atia, who by that time had nimbly jumped out of harm's way.

He bobbed and weaved away from the outstretched arms as the creature made its last clawing grabs. Finally it slammed heavily to the ground, and the whole area seemed to shake with its impact.

It lay on its side, absolutely still and completely silent.

Atia stood several yards away, not moving, and watched the big Neanderthal. He was ready to leap away if the Neanderthal should so much as twitch a single muscle.

Its eyes were still open and staring at him, but after a few more seconds had passed, Atia saw that they were beginning to glaze over. Atia recognized this as the first sign of death, but he still hesitated to get closer to the fallen man-thing.

His hunting knife was still embedded in the Neanderthal's chest, and he knew that he had to retrieve it, but he hesitated.

A quick look at Avoti, who was still fighting for his very life with the active Neanderthal opponent, strengthened Atia's resolve. He dashed in closer to the unmoving body, and with a great pull tore the knife free. Without thinking, Atia immediately jumped back and away from the body.

Atia was now able to tum his attention back to Avoti, whom he saw had listened to his quickly given instructions.

The shouted instructions were to keep the second huge Neanderthal busy, to keep out of its way, and not to exchange any sword strokes with him.

It would have been comical if things were not so serious. There was Avoti literally running in circles, first in one direction and then in the other.

This, of course, was being done to keep the big man -thing's attention from Atia in order to give him the time he needed to deal with his own Neanderthal problem.

An exhausted Avoti happily removed himself out of harm's way when he saw Atia running rapidly toward him.

He flipped the sword that he was using up in the air, which allowed Atia to grab it and go into an on -guard position as the Neanderthal turned its attention to him.

Atia lifted the sword and the blade clashed with that of his enemy's. The high-pitched sound was completely lost in the echoes of the icy landscape that surrounded them.

Atia knew that he was the faster of the two of them, but this beast-man also had the great advantage of superior strength.

Strangely, Atia and his large opponent seemed to be evenly matched with their swords in their hands.

For every quality stroke Atia made, his enemy seemed able to counterstrike and make most of his own major moves with practiced ease.

This meant that the Neanderthal must have had a great deal of experience fighting humans. It was apparent, since he was definitely still alive, that he must have been successful against the smaller but quicker opposition.

Atia immediately realized that he had to be extremely careful and treat this giant with the greatest of respect when it came to his swordplay.

Atia had never fought against such an enemy with sword before, either human or Neanderthal.

Amazingly it seemed that they both knew the exact same techniques and were both masters of identical tactics. It was as though they had both been instructed by exactly the same tutors.

As their swords rang together, Atia felt his strength beginning to desert him. The stronger strokes that he had to defend against from the powerful Neanderthal were rapidly weakening him.

He knew that he could not win by strength alone, because he could never hope to match the terrible might of the giant enemy who was now facing him with a large and most evil smile on his ugly face. The only route to a victory that seemed open to him was for Atia to do something he had never done before, and that was for him to adopt a completely new and different technique and strategy. He knew that he had no other chance to win this battle of swords unless he quickly developed a new and tricky approach.

But his opponent gave him few, if any, openings. The Neanderthal gave him nothing that he could capitalize on.

In a matter of a few minutes, when Atia's sword arm would tire and begin to falter, he would need to have a plan already set in his mind and ready to go.

As Atia parried like a fencer, then tried bludgeoning like a barbarian warrior against his much bigger opponent, an idea came to him. He thought of a dangerous but very doable tactic that he could adopt. It was something that he had never tried before. He hoped never to be in a situation again that would require something so desperate.

If it did not work out, then he knew that he was a dead man. His son would be stuck in these wastelands without him, and he would be facing this same killer Neanderthal.

He lifted his left hand and ripped off the huge medallion that he wore. It had the Bear Clan insignia on it.

He threw it into the face of the beast-man, who was distracted for only an instant as he looked up at the thrown shiny object. That one moment of distraction was all that Atia needed.

He lashed out strongly with his right foot and, putting whatever strength he had left into that kick, caught the unsuspecting Neanderthal directly in his crotch.

Atia had assumed that, man or beast-man, when hit with a

sudden blow to his manhood he would have a few moments of weakness. This was what Atia put his own life and the life of his son on the line for.

If this mountain of a man-thing could shrug off that hard blow to his balls, then Atia knew that he was a dead man.

Down went his enemy, who had instinctively dropped his sword and fallen heavily to the ground, holding onto his vital area with both hands.

Quickly Atia was on top of him, with the same twelve-inch blade that he had used upon the other Neanderthal.

This time the enemy's neck was open to his thrust, and with all of his remaining strength he plunged the entire length of the long knife into the unguarded neck of his fallen opponent.

The same red-green blood gushed out of the neck of the now-dead Neanderthal. Atia did a quick jump backward to avoid the blood that poured out of the gaping wound.

An utterly exhausted Atia dropped to the ground and waited for his son to join him.

# CHAPTER TWENTY-THREE

everal weeks had passed, and Atia was almost feeling like his old self again.

The experience that his son Avoti and he had had with the two Neanderthals was now becoming just an unpleasant memory that the two of them had shared.

Atia had talked with the elders of the tribe. They all agreed that they needed to do something about the Neanderthals, and they needed to do it as soon as possible.

Recently they had lost a large hunting party that had been surrounded and attacked by Neanderthals. The humans never had a chance.

Everyone decided to wait until Atia had healed and would be able to get involved with the leadership again before they discussed what they could do.

In the meantime Atia had called for an evening gathering with all of the people from the tribe. It was to be a campfire meeting where they would all sit around eating treats and special cuts of meat that the tribal women were to prepare.

The plan was for both young and older members of the tribe to get to know each other better and listen to stories told by the adult members.

The children ranged from age five to early teenagers, and it was a good time for all. The adults, both men and women, shared their favorite stories about something that had happened to them.

This was one of the usual bonding events that the tribe held every so often to let the younger and older people interact with each other to achieve a good comfort level.

Atia had asked if he could be the last speaker of the evening. He slowly stood up and looked around to see if he had everyone's attention.

His glance took him over to where his son Avoti was sitting beside the special girl that he had told Atia about.

Avoti was almost fourteen years old and just getting to realize his early manhood. He had only recently become aware that, in addition to his male friends, there were young females hanging around.

There was one girl who was always smiling at him lately, and Avoti found himself smiling back.

Atia was aware of the fact that Avoti was old enough now to be taught about sex and the proper way to go about these things.

In the tribe, one of the older, single and unattached females would take a week off from her other tribal duties and invite a young and sexually aware male teenager to spend some time alone with her in the nearby wooded area, where she promised to introduce him to the amazing adventure of sex.

Atia could only smile to himself when he thought about his own wonderful week that he had spent with Chotel when they went off together into the forest.

Chotel was an older woman of twenty-four who had recently lost her mate in one of the attacks that the Neanderthals had made on the clan.

She was very pleased to be with Atia as they spent their time hunting, talking and personally exploring the absolute wonders of sex.

Atia remembered that he came back to the tribe feeling that he was now truly a man. He looked at all the females in the tribe with a different view and an interested attitude. How simple life was for him in those days.

Atia cleared his throat in order to get everyone's attention. He said that he wanted to speak about two subjects and that he would try to be brief.

He bent down carefully and took one of the burning branches from out of the central fire pit. The branch was sizzling and burning brightly from the animal fat that had dripped upon it from the cooking meat.

"Without fire," he began, "our tribe would not be here at all.

We would be no better off than the wild animals that we hunt. If we did not have fire, how could we cook our food or warm ourselves when we were cold? What would keep the wild animals away from us if there were no fires to protect us?

"Everyone knows that we need three things to make a fire. We need a spark from a firestone such as a flint, which we all carry with us, something to burn like this wooden branch, and open air to start the flame and keep the fire burning.

I think that we can all agree that having fire is a good thing for all of us.

"Now, our ancestors did not have fire to help them in those early days. They would call upon their gods to help them survive in the difficult world that they lived in without having fire that we have now.

"As we all now know, there is a god for everything. There is a fire god, a sun god, a rain god, a god for hunting, and a god for everything else. But our early people had no fire and they prayed every day to a god to help them.

These special gods of ours are called the Titans, which in our language means a special race of giant gods who rule our world from their palace in the sky above us all."

"I am going to talk to you now about only two special Titans who watch over us. One is a sad story, and one is an exciting and adventurous story.

The sad story is about one of mankind's most helpful Titans/ gods. His name is Prometheus.

But before I get into my story, I want you all to understand a few things about the gods who are watching us every day.

Titans/gods are very dangerous and very mysterious. They have mighty powers and can cast spells with nothing more than a special gesture or a special word.

Together these Titans control all of the forces of nature and mankind in the world. But even though they control all things, they usually stay at home where they live doing their own special things.

Most of them live alone and away from each other as most of them do not get along. So they, pretty much, stay to themselves and do not bother with mankind.

"Now here are a few very important facts as I personally understand them about these special Titans/gods.

The Titans were brought to life by Mother Earth and Father Sky. They are immortal giants of incredible strength and size. There are twelve known Titans.

It is one of these twelve Titans who is of the utmost importance to us as human beings. His name is Prometheus. He was the one god who looked down at humanity from his place in the sky and took pity on the hard life that was forced upon us as we lived without fire.

The other Titans/gods told him 'no' when he asked them to help him give the gift of fire to humans. The other eleven Titans did not care about us very much.

So, Prometheus went against every other Titan and came down from the heavens to teach our people how to create and use fire for our everyday needs.

The king of the Titans was so angry with Prometheus for not

listening to him that he had the other gods help him with a swift and terrible punishment against Prometheus.

"Prometheus was sentenced by the king of the gods to spend the rest of his long life in eternal torture chained to a large rock where each day an eagle was sent to attack him and feed on his liver.

Each night Prometheus would heal and the liver would grow back again and be whole until the eagle came back to attack him again and again.

This went on for generations. Prometheus' screams of pain were so loud and violent that they caused earthquakes all over our entire continent.

"The good part of this sad story is that the great hero Hercules finally set him free many generations later.

We believe that he did so because Hercules, who was part human and part Titan himself, could not stand the idea of an eagle doing such a terrible thing to another Titan.

"And now before I go on with my second and final Titan/god story about my own personal favorite Titan, named Mars, I want to tell you what our holy men say that the home of the gods looks like.

They tell us that there is a place filled with silver and gold towers with sweeping green terraces everywhere. It has wide walkways surrounded by thousands of gold and red flowers and the air is always sweet and clean.

And now let me finish my final point of interest and tell you about my favorite Titan of them all, and by now you know I am talking about Mars, the god of war.

"It was my personal tribute to Mars that saved my mate Ava's life. It was during the great flood that wiped out her clan and brought us both here to you where we have learned to love you all.

My titan/god, called Mars, is second in power and strength to the supreme head of all the gods, named Zeus.

My special god, Mars, is thought to be a great warrior. His manner is very calm and levelheaded except during times of war.

During war times, he goes on a violent rampage that no one, god or human, can stand up against.

"Mars is the defender of our clan and of our whole tribe.

He is known to favor the wolf because the wolf is smart and cunning. He also favors the woodpecker.

I personally do not understand why Mars would have picked the woodpecker, but then again, I am not a god, and so, I do not have any insight into this strange choice.

Mars, as I have just said, is my personal god to whom I pray each and every night before I go to sleep.

"And speaking of sleep, here is my last bedtime story for all of you young ones.

I had a special dream the other night. I was in the far end of a huge cave. It was too dark inside for me to see anything very clearly. But what I was able to see was what looked like a huge bright red lantern far above me. It was coming closer and closer.

I was finally able to make out a great shadow of a nose under that huge red lantern and, finally, I saw the bright gleam of huge teeth.

"I suddenly realized that the lantern that I was looking at was one great big flaming eye, and that eye belonged to a giant whom we call a Cyclops, a race of giants who all have only one eye in the middle of their foreheads.

I was able to make out clearly the whole large figure standing there before me. I saw that it was a giant who was as tall as a tree. His huge fingers reaching out of the shadows were as big as branches.

Those fingers closed around two nearby companions of mine and pulled them up and away as they went screaming into the air.

"As I watched, the giant's hands carried the struggling little men into his mouth, where he began to eat them, still wiggling, the way a cat will eat a grasshopper. He ate them clothes and all, growling and smacking his lips over their raw bones. They must have been a special treat for him.

"That is what Titans look like.

"And now, off to bed with all of you children. I want to wish you all a good night's sleep without any nightmares."

# CHAPTER TWENTY-FOUR

Mog was not feeling very safe and secure in his leadership of the newly formed Neanderthal army. He had been hearing several rumors, and they all involved the former second-in-command of the army, General Ping. Ping was said not to be happy about being asked to leave his command position after the death of Leader Snark.

This all happened after the now-famous wrestling match to the death between Mog and his former boss Leader Snark.

It was told to Mog by his internal spy system that many Neanderthal officers in Mog's newly formed army still felt a great deal of loyalty to General Ping and not to Mog himself.

Mog knew that he had to do something about this potentially dangerous situation, and he finally came up with a plan that he immediately put into motion.

His key to what he hoped would be a successful plot that he was hatching revolved around his special live-in human female slave Kat. He knew that she would go along with any plot or killing that he, Mog, thought necessary.

That evening after a quiet dinner in their animal-hide tent, Mog took Kat out for a walk around the campsite. They were followed at a respectful distance by two specially trained bodyguards hired by Mog to always shadow him wherever he went. Mog believed in being careful, and if anyone such as General Ping or any other of his many enemies had ideas of assassinating him, these two bodyguards would be invaluable assets to his personal safety.

The conversation was dominated by Mog, who questioned Kat as to how things were going with finding smart human female slaves. These female slaves would have to be willing to take orders as officers in the newly formed armed forces under Kat's control.

Kat told him that she was having a very difficult time finding females who had any fighting spirit left after having been beaten and raped over and over again by their Neanderthal captors.

She wisely suggested that Mog set up a procedure where Kat could buy the females and make them part of Mog's household so that they could avoid being sold off to male Neanderthals. Mog agreed to allow her to screen the human females before they went on the slave block. He felt that she was absolutely correct. What he wanted and needed were females who still had some fighting spirit left in them.

Moving on from that discussion point, he brought up the rumors that he was hearing about General Ping. Kat also thought that she had heard something or other about the same thing.

Mog then went on and explained his thoughts about how to rid them of the hateful and very dangerous general.

There was much laughter and excitement in Kat's voice as she added her thoughts to Mog's plot to get rid of the general. She knew that her reward would be wonderful if everything went according to plan.

After much back-and-forth discussion, they finally came up with the final solution for eliminating him.

𒁹 𒐲 𒐚𒁹

Several weeks later, Mog, according to the master plan, had had several late afternoon meetings with General Ping.

Mog told General Ping that he wanted to hear whatever thoughts and ideas that Ping would bring to the army if he were asked to once again resume his second -in-command position under Mog.

At first the general was a non-believer; even though he accepted the meeting with Mog, he had several of his own personal bodyguards waiting just outside the tent where they held their one-on-one talks.

The meeting, scheduled for later that special afternoon, was somewhat different from the plan agreed upon by Mog and Kat.

Mog had invited the general to a social evening with himself and one of his favorite female human slaves, Kat.

The general had seen Kat moving freely around the camp for the past several months, and the look of her had excited him into accepting the date once Mog explained that there would be a sexual threesome. This threesome would be made up of the two of them and his human female slave, Kat.

When the special day arrived and the sun was starting to set in the sky, Mog had a dinner set up for the general's bodyguards in an adjacent tent.

It was in the plan to get the general to think more about Kat's body than his own life. This allowed the general to accept having his bodyguards' dinner served to them at a distance away from where Mog's sex party was going to be held. If the general had known that the dinner and wine being served to his bodyguards would quickly and quietly kill them, then things would have turned out differently.

The sound of her shoes clanked on the shiny wooden floor as Kat, alone, entered the room that was commonly known by the household staff as "Mog's Passion Pit".

A soft glow emanated from inside the large tent as she entered the room. What she saw was a lovely living area with a huge bed set up against one of the far sides and two very comfortable Neanderthal-sized chairs on each side of the bed. There were two more chairs in the far corner.

Kat closed the tent flap as she noted to herself that her chosen companions for the evening had not arrived

Several vases of flowers adorned the room and the smell of them filled the entire area. She was very pleased with the setting; she would compliment the serving staff later.

The location was set and the play-acting would shortly begin. She knew the evening's script by heart, having played the scene over and over in her mind many times.

Usually Mog would pick some very pretty but poor human serving girl from outside the camp. He would promise her several gold pieces, and the girl was always very pleased to spend the afternoon with them.

It did not bother Kat at all when Mog brought in a female human as the third player or if Mog spent an extra amount of his time with the visitor and less time with her. Kat was a good sport about it, and she, too, enjoyed touching and fondling this other woman.

Every so often Mog would surprise her with a Neanderthal soldier from out of the local army group.

Whenever this happened, Kat had a double dose of excitement.

She would then have the thrill of two males doing all those wonderful things to her body, and she would see Mog kill the unsuspecting soldier right before her eyes.

The soldier had to die because they could not have him talking about what was going on inside Mog's private quarters.

Kat understood all that, but what was so wonderful about being an eyewitness to a murder was the sex that followed with

Mog, one on one. The sex was more thrilling than anything else she had experienced in her young life, and she had experienced quite a bit already.

Tonight was different. Tonight she had personally been involved in solving the problem with Mog.

She had offered up her body as the solution, and Mog had accepted her suggestion.

More and more she found Mog depending upon her for a second opinion on a full range of topics. As Mog always said, she was not just another pretty face.

After tonight's death of the bodyguards, and then of General Ping, Mog would have no one to worry about, and he could do as he pleased with the Neanderthal army.

As Mog's woman, her place in the social setting of the army base would be second to no one except Mog himself. She was extremely satisfied with the way things had worked out for her.

Now here she was, sitting in this special room, waiting for the evening to develop and running all these things through her mind, when she heard the opening act of the play, beginning with the sound of the pulled tent entry flap.

She heard Mog's deep voice saying, "I've missed you, Kat. I've missed you very much."

She smiled as she looked in his direction.

Another deep voice came from behind Mog. "I've missed you a lot, too, my dear young lady."

# CHAPTER TWENTY-FIVE

Both Neanderthal men crossed the room, and each sat down in one of the chairs that were facing Kat by the side of the bed. Hot flashes were suddenly whirling through her body as she sat there. This was going to be something exciting for her once again.

Under Mog's watchful eye she had had sex with one human male many times and with two human males several times. She had once had sex with one Neanderthal and one human male at the same time. But this time she was going to do it with two Neanderthal males at the same time. The last time Mog had made her do it with two Neanderthal males, she had been uncomfortable, but maybe this time it would be easier. If this plan of theirs did not kill her, she might just really enjoy it.

Mog, who was getting into the spirit of the moment, moved in front of her, knelt down and took her small hand in his.

His brown eyes glittered in the candlelight. It was the warmth of love or the pretense of love shining from his face that melted her heart for that one special moment.

"Kat, I love you. I always have and I always will. I love having you in my life."

His soft breath brushed across the back of her hand as he

kissed it, sending tingles through her. Mog was really into the full spirit of it.

"Yes," she answered, hardly able to catch her breath.

He stood up quickly, pulled her up into his strong arms and kissed her softly on her waiting lips. He then released her to sit on the edge of the bed once again.

To her surprise General Ping took Mog's place and went through the exact same play-acting, using the exact same words.

Kat now understood that Mog had told the general to do whatever he did because the general was probably not smart enough to think up his own lines.

Both men were now standing, and they took off their outer clothing. All that they were left wearing were tight black leather pants that were army regulation issue.

Kat stood up and she, too, removed her covering.

Both Neanderthal men took in deep breaths as they looked at her standing there proudly showing them her well-formed young firm body. She was wearing her shoes and a wide smile, and that was all that she really needed.

She knew that she was beautiful, and she put her hands under each of her breasts and pushed them up and out toward the Neanderthals. The nipples were hard, and red in color. This was her own personal way of offering herself to the two of them.

General Ping looked at Mog, who nodded, and they both went up to her. Each one took one of her arms and gently lifted her off her feet. They placed her in the middle of the large bed and sat down beside her, one of them on each side of her. They were still holding onto her arms so that she could not move while they each began to suck and fondle the large breast that was on their side.

The sensations running through her....

She made a hopeless half-hearted attempt to move but had no real desire to resist.

She was absolutely loving the double pleasure that she was

receiving. She felt herself beginning to burn up with internal heat, and she was hoping that they would bring her to a climax soon because the pressure she was feeling internally was almost unbearable.

Each of them took a long and slender piece of rope from the pocket of their leather pants and tied one end around her wrist and the other to the headboard at the top of the bed.

She would be able to move her head from side to side and move her lower body quite freely, but that was all that was allowed to her.

Mog unfastened his black leather pants and drew out his erection. As he stepped to the side of the bed, Kat opened her mouth and took the full length of him into her mouth as she began to rock her head back and forth.

The general noted that this was something that she must have done before. No one could take in that much without a gagging sensation taking over. Kat had, obviously, overcome this problem with lots of practice. The look on Mog's face was one of pure pleasure.

The general, in the meantime, had also removed his black leather pants, and he, too, stood naked with a huge erection leading him. The general saw that it was time for him to get into the game.

Kat was still going strong with Mog, so her attention was fully on him and away from the general.

He positioned himself between her thrashing legs and entered her quite easily. She seemingly was sexually stimulated, and she was well lubricated internally as he went in quickly and deeply.

Kat did not slow down her mouth's working on Mog as the general roughly banged away at her.

He had no need to be gentle with her, and he had to admit that he was having a great time sticking it to the young and beautiful female human.

This was very exciting for the general. He was really enjoying himself as Mog's guest. Perhaps he should look at Leader Mog in a completely different light. Any Neanderthal who would share a human female such as this one must be given the benefit of the doubt. Maybe the two of them could get along after all. It was worth thinking about.

The general finished with a gasp and climbed down. He went over to the chair where he had left his leather pants. He was not comfortable walking around without any clothing on, so he quickly got dressed. The general just sat there and watched the couple finish.

When Mog was done, he also walked over to his chair and put his leather pants back on.

Kat was still lying there trying to get her strength back. Her hands were still secured to the headboard and she was making soft sounds. The general could not decide if it was pleasure or pain that she was expressing. He really didn't care, and it really didn't matter.

The general got up after his breathing had completely returned to normal and walked over to the still-heavily breathing Mog.

The general told him that he had to take a bathroom break and, if Mog didn't want the lady to cool down while he was gone, suggested that Mog continue to stroke her breasts to keep her going. Her breasts seemed to be her most sensitive spots, and that was where she seemed to like being touched.

The general watched Mog walk over and sit down as he began to play with the generous breast waiting for him on his side of the bed.

The general then turned his back on them and went out the rear-flapping door on the way to the nearby outdoor bathroom.

Mog quickly jumped off the bed. He took an extra moment and gave the breast on the other side of Kat's wiggling body a little squeeze. Mog always enjoyed being an "equal squeezer."

Mog positioned himself on the side of the same flap that the general had gone out of so that when he returned, the general would have to take one full step into the room before he could see the bed.

What he would see was the moving figure of the human but

not Mog. Before the general could react to that, Mog would have his chance.

Long moments passed and finally the door opened. The general took his first step into the room. He must have instantly sensed that something was wrong because he started to tum back toward the open-door flap when Mog pounced.

With all his great strength behind it, Mog threw his best right hook to the chin of the turning general, who took the blow straight on. The general was knocked out before he started to fall to the floor.

Mog dropped the long bladed knife that he was holding in his left hand. He needed both hands free for what he was about to do. He took the general's head with one hand and his shoulders with the other and twisted with all his strength.

A very satisfying *crack* told Mog that he had broken the neck of this Neanderthal.

He checked for a heartbeat and found none. He also checked his pulse and found none. The Neanderthal was definitely dead.

The only thing left to do was to give Mog's human female slave his final shot of the day. He had enjoyed thinking about this part of the plan, and he knew that he would enjoy this final part as much as he had enjoyed breaking the general's neck.

Mog carefully unbound Kat's raw wrists from the ropes that held them in place. He never spoke a word as he turned her over onto her hands and knees.

The female was well trained and she immediately took up the proper position of putting her weight on her arms, leaning forward and lifting up her rear end with her slender legs nicely spread out.

He entered her slowly and carefully. He knew that she must have been very sore from all the abuse she had taken to her sexual organs. He reached forward and played with her beautiful breasts for the last time that evening.

Like all males, Neanderthal or human, he was a breast man, and Kat had one of the finest sets he had ever been allowed to touch.

He continued to pump into this woman, going deeper and deeper until he was in as far as he could go. Minutes later he was done, and he pulled himself off the woman and pulled up his black leather pants.

He went out the front door to tell the household maids to attend to their mistress and to have them call someone to get rid of the general's body.

He walked away into the clear, crisp night thinking that all was now right with the world. He had plans to make and a world to conquer.

# CHAPTER TWENTY-SIX

Supreme Leader Atia and three other leaders of the newly formed human army were sitting comfortably around the small campfire that looked down on the flat training grounds where soldiers were moving about.

There were several hours left until sunset, and the soldiers were scattered all over the area working on their fighting skills as they took their orders from their officers.

The leaders were listening to a detailed report from General Tukk as to how things were going with the new formations.

His words were spoken in his usual deep and calm voice that fit his role as senior commander of the foot soldiers.

The army was broken up into three separate parts with General Tukk as infantry commander, General Ladd as archery commander, and General Mann as cavalry commander.

The three generals all reported to Atia, who was the Supreme Leader.

General Tukk told them his foot soldiers had been experimenting with new formation groups that had never been tried before.

If what was being done on the practice field could hold up under battlefield conditions, then he promised to have the Neanderthals on the defensive for the first time.

"It is the purpose of our military strategy to diminish the possibility of resistance from the enemy," General Tukk said. "And our enemies, the Neanderthals, are bigger and stronger than we are. In a one-on-one fight with one of our soldiers, we lose most of the time. Let me repeat myself1 In a one-on-one-fight with one of our soldiers, we usually lose.

"The common-sense answer to this is to avoid a one-on-one confrontation. This is easy to say, but until now we have had no way to get around it.

"Our new strategy, therefore, is based on the position that we will only fight the enemy in groups and never as individuals.

"The standing order will be if one or more of our people encounter one or more of theirs, we must turn around and get the hell out of there. Of course, our men won't like running from the enemy, but a dead human soldier is no good to us, and we will drill this into their heads. They must learn to turn and run away so that

| 1 0 0   M E N | |
|---|---|
| 1 | 1 |
| 0 | 0 |
| 0 | 0 |
| M | M |
| E | E |
| N | N |
| 1 0 0   M E N | |

they can live to fight another day.

"Now let me turn your attention to the gray parchment that I have given to you. This is page one of three pages. Page two is the yellow one and page three is the soft red color. What you are looking at on page one is a simple square which represents a four-sided figure with one-hundred armed men standing next to each other on each of the four sides. This makes a total of four hundred men."

"Surrounding this small square of four hundred men is a square identical to the first one except that it

*is* larger. It is made up of one-hundred-fifty men

standing next to each other. This fighting square will have a total of six-hundred highly mobile and deadly fighting men."

"Pages one and two show you two squares. As I have said, the first square will have one-hundred men on each side which is a total of four-hundred men and square two will have one-hundred-fifty

| 1 5 0   M E N | | |
|---|---|---|
| 1 | | 1 |
| 5 | | 5 |
| 0 | | 0 |
| | | |
| M | | M |
| E | | E |
| N | | N |
| 1 5 0   M E N | | |

men to a side which is a total of six hundred men. The combined total is one thousand men for each fighting square."

"Please look at page three's drawing showing the bigger square surrounding and protecting the smaller square inside it."

| 1 5 0   M E N | | | | |
|---|---|---|---|---|
| 1 | | 1 0 0 M E N | | 1 |
| 5 | 1 | | 1 | 5 |
| 0 | 0 | | 0 | 0 |
| | 0 | | 0 | |
| M | M | | M | M |
| E | E | | E | E |
| N | N | 1 0 0 M E N | N | N |
| | | 1 5 0   M E N | | |

"The way that this works is that the outer square of men is holding well-balanced, exceptionally long, razor sharp pointed spears. These special spears, of course, are much longer than any spears that the enemy will have. The longer spears will keep the enemy away while the inner square of soldiers will continuously stand there and shoot arrow after arrow into the ranks of the enemy who can not get at them due to the protection provided for them by the outer square of spear holders. Those arrows will be shot nonstop at the enemy, and they will have a terrible effect on them because the enemy will not be able to get to our archers due to the safety provided by the outer square's protection."

"This is a very simple and very deadly way of destroying our enemy without exposing our men to the enemy at all. In addition to the extremely long and well balanced spears that our troops in the outer square will be holding, they will each be carrying an oversized shield that they will all put over their heads to protect them from any arrows that the enemy might shower down on them."

"The absolute beauty of this 'fighting square', is that in perfectly trained movements, they will be able to walk right up into the thickest of the enemy forces and, with almost perfect immunity, shoot hundreds of arrows into the opposition without having any return fire coming back at them from the enemy."

T III⊩ ⅓T

The council of four leaders looked down at the flat area below them and watched in perfect silence as several of the fighting squares worked on their walking and coordination skills.

They were all amazed and pleased to see that so many men could be taught to work together into these efficient killing machines.

# CHAPTER TWENTY-SEVEN

With a big smile on his face, Atia acknowledged the general's strong and uplifting report on the progress that the foot-soldier division of the armed forces was achieving.

General Ladd, head of the archer and spear-thrower division, began speaking next.

"Gentlemen," the general began to speak in such a soft voice that each of the three listeners had to lean forward in order to hear what he was saying. "The archery and spear division of our army was having some major problems up to about a year ago.

"It appears that the Neanderthals got their hands on some of our bows and arrows, and they began to make their own weapons, based on these samples.

"As we all know, the enemy is bigger and stronger than we are so they had to thicken the base of their imitation bows and then they had to triple the thickness of the bow strings because of their big hands.

"Thank the gods that this meant that the arrow that they can shoot from their copycat bow and arrow will not go as far as an arrow that our warriors can shoot.

"By actual measure, our bow will let an arrow fly about an

# ATIA: BRONZE AGE WARRIOR

extra ten yards beyond what the enemy can fire back at us. Now this ten yards might not sound like a lot of distance to you, but if our men can be taught to stay at least ten yards out of the range of incoming Neanderthal arrows, then we have a definite winner here.

"Let me explain this very important fact another way.

"If an enemy archer were to shoot their arrow at us, and the maximum distance that their arrow could fly was, let us say, two hundred yards, all our archers would have to do would be to stay two hundred and ten yards away from them.

"We can shoot back at them, and our arrow would fly into them at the longer distance of two hundred and ten yards. We would hit our target but the Neanderthal arrows would land ten yards in front of our archers."

"As good as this advantage of ten yards is, I have something to report that is even better."

"Our weapon makers have come up with something that they call a 'longbow'. This is a bow that is six inches longer and, with proper practice, can be shot, with the same deadly accuracy, about an additional fifteen yards. This is most important. We already have a ten -yard advantage with our old bow but, with this new longbow, we gain another fifteen yards. This means that we can now keep our archers the extra distance away from the enemy, where we can hit them but they cannot hit us back."

"We have already started making the new longbow, and my best guess is that in about one year from now all of our archers will be longbow shooters."

"My second and final report on weapons is about an improvement in an area where we always lost to the Neanderthals every time our spear men went up against their spear men."

"Due to the extra strength that the Neanderthals have over our warriors, they were always able to throw their spear at us with great accuracy and hit us about twenty yards farther than we could hit them. I am pleased to tell you now that in about the same timeframe of one year we will have produced what we are calling a 'spear thrower.' This spear thrower will allow us to get that extra twenty yards back that we always lost to the enemy. This will allow us to hold our own in a spear-throwing fight."

"Let me explain how this works. It is quite simple. The new invention, a spear thrower as I mentioned, is a simple leather throng attached to a leather pouch that gives extra speed to a thrown spear."

"A regular, ordinary spear is put into the pouch which will add that extra distance we were always short. We will be able to match spear throw for spear throw within the same time frame of about one year."

General Ladd smiled and sat down with a satisfied look on his face.

The final speaker was General Mann, who now stood up and nodded politely to each of his fellows.

"My report is on our newly formed cavalry unit. We have never had a horse-riding soldier before. This is a first for us. As we all know, the Neanderthals are much bigger than any human when on foot. However, if we mount a man on a horse, then the weight advantage comes over to us.

"Horses live on grass and we do not have to worry about feeding them. With a horse, we can get to any place on the battlefield quickly. The horse can be trained to run right over our enemy or bring us to where we want to go quicker than ever before."

"These horses are very strong and they seem to be intelligent and easy to train. They can carry great weights for us and take them a great distance. Horses will increase our mobility, and I see a great future in a partnership between horses and humans."

Atia stood and thanked the general for his most interesting report.

"Gentlemen," he began, "It should be the aim of every leader to discover the weaknesses of the enemy and to take advantage of those weaknesses."

"Based upon your reports today, and what I have seen going on all around us, I believe our ultimate victory is not in doubt. Time will be our ally only when we get these new weapons into the hands of our soldiers."

"But here is the biggest problem as I see it. We will win the local war against the local Neanderthals, but we can't allow any of them to survive anywhere in the world."

"They will always be a threat to mankind. I am afraid that when this local war is over, we will have to go on a worldwide expedition in our war of extermination."

"It will be many years and possibly generations from now that humans will have to wipe out the Neanderthals once and for all. In that way we can preserve our continent for our children and their children who will follow them."

"Unless there is something further that anyone wants to bring up, I will close this important meeting."

"I have to take a ride with General Ladd who came across something that he tells me I need to see."

"Thank you, generals, and I wish you all the very best."

# CHAPTER TWENTY-EIGHT

Winter was gasping its last frozen breath, reluctantly giving way to spring, but the youthful season was capricious.

Amid the many frigid reminders of glacial chill, tantalizing hints of warmth promised summer heat to the entire area.

The two men were traveling with reflections of a dazzling sun glinting from patches of snow and ice along the way, with a sky that was a deep and radiant blue.

Ragged tatters of clouds streamed far to the south of where the two horses were carefully picking their way. They were following a medium-sized stream of water whose course was fairly straight and slightly downhill, making the going easy.

They saw flecks of green on the brush near the banks of the stream, and they saw occasional small flowers bravely poking their miniature faces through the melting patches of snow.

The huge mountain range was a barrier to the harsh glacial winds and the maritime breezes off the distant sea. It warmed and watered the narrow strip and south -facing slopes into a temperate climate.

It was a surprised Atia who had to pull his horse to a stop when General Ladd drew his horse to a standstill.

The general had guided them to the side of a small hilly area where he dismounted and motioned to Atia to do the same.

Atia followed him for perhaps a dozen or more paces on foot until they came to a flat area that was half filled with gravel and sand.

The general halted and waited as Atia walked up to him.

"What is it?" Atia asked.

The general turned and faced Atia, his eyes were narrow and his jaw was tight. He unfastened his cloak and undid his sword and placed them on a nearby rock.

"Get rid of your cloak and your weapons," he said. "They will only get in the way."

Atia had an idea of what was coming, and he decided he had better go along with it. He removed his cloak and put it, along with his weapons, next to the general's on the same rock.

"Ladd, it's your play. What's on your mind?"

"It's been a very long time now since my brother Dal's death. I am not saying that his death was caused by you, but I am not fully satisfied that you didn't have something to do with it."

"I just thought that we should have a man-to-man rough-and-tumble just to remind you of who I am and to make sure that you know that I will be watching you. I will be watching you very carefully."

He came at Atia slowly, as Atia got his own fists out in front of him and backed away a few steps.

He was much bigger than Atia but probably not as fast.

Atia realized that he really had no choice but to face him now rather than having an enemy somewhere lurking behind him in the future.

He thought to himself that it was very strange how certain things come back to haunt you if you give them enough time to develop.

The general's brother Dal was killed in the flood that wiped out the lives of everyone except for his mate, Ava. That was on the day that the volcano exploded and tremendous amounts of water came down from the mountaintop, washing out the entire valley.

In his mind Atia clearly recalled that day of the cave bear. The strange thing was that he, Atia, had had absolutely nothing to do with Dal's death. It was true that he had made love to Ava, who was Dal's mate at the time, but he did not cause the death of the general's brother.

Both of the men crouched, and the general was making slow punching movements with his left hand, as if he was getting ready to come at Atia.

In the past if Atia ever had to fight against anyone, it would never have been his choice to do so with his hands. If he had to fight with someone like the general, his choice of special weapons would have been a sword or quarterstaff.

These weapons would have given him a chance to use his speed and strategy and given him a chance to wear down his opponent.

Atia brushed away the general's half-hearted punches a few times, as he stepped up his movements and pressed nearer to Atia with every step.

Finally Atia saw an opening, ducked under the general's jab, and swung a hard left that landed a little above his middle. That blow would have broken a stout board or ruptured the insides of a lesser mortal than the general. Atia only got a grunt as a response to his blow, and at the same time the general blocked his follow-up blow. He pushed his right hand under Atia's left arm, catching his shoulder from behind. Atia closed with him quickly, anticipating a shoulder lock that he might not have been able to get out of.

Atia turned, driving forward and catching the general's left shoulder in a similar fashion. He hooked his right leg behind the general's knee and was able to cast him backward to the ground.

The general maintained his firm grip on Atia and pulled him down with him.

Atia had to release his own hold and was only able to drive his right elbow into the general's left side as they both hit the ground together.

For a moment Atia had a clear shot at the general's groin with his right hand, but he restrained himself. It was not that he had any qualms about hitting a man below the belt, but he held back. He knew that if he had hit the general right then, the general's reflexes to the blow would cause him to break Atia's shoulder, since he still had a firm grip on it. Instead of a low blow, Atia, rubbing his forearm on the gravel, managed to twist his left arm between his legs, catching the general above his left thigh.

Atia rolled back, attempting to straighten his legs as soon as his feet were beneath him. He wanted to raise the general off the ground and slam him back down and then stomp on him.

The general would allow none of this; with one great heave, he tore himself free and leaped backward.

The two of them were separated. The general was the aggressor again and started moving toward Atia. It was probably his intention to maul Atia with his greater strength, and that thought made Atia decide to take a few chances.

He watched the general's feet and, at what he judged to be the best moment, dove beneath his extended arms. Just as he was shifting his weight forward onto his left foot, Atia was able to catch hold of his right ankle. By lifting it he caused the general to fall backward.

As Ladd scrambled to get to his feet, Atia caught the general on the jaw with a strong right hook that knocked him down again.

He shook his big head to clear it as he came back at Atia one more time.

Atia tried to put him down with a direct kick to the stomach, but the general turned sideways and the kick bounced off his hip.

The general regained his balance and advanced at Atia once again. Atia threw several jabs to his face and a quick right to his stomach. He felt as if he were fighting against an immovable and unstoppable body.

He knew that he was in real trouble, as nothing that he could do seemed able to slow the general down.

The general smiled.

He knew that Atia was afraid to close with him. As Atia snapped a kick at his stomach and connected, his arms came down a bit and Atia was able to chop him alongside the neck just above the collar bone.

At that moment, the general's arms shot forward and locked about Atia's waist. Atia slammed his jaw with the heel of his hand, but it did not stop him from tightening his grip as he raised Atia above the ground.

It was too late for Atia to hit him again.

Atia sought out the carotids in his neck and squeezed as hard as he could. This, also, did not slow the general down.

The general raised Atia high up over his head and slammed him down on his back in the gravel.

There were bursting points of light in his head, and the world was a jittering, half-real place, as the general dragged Atia to his feet.

Atia saw the big fist coming at his face, and there was nothing that he could do about it.

The fight was over at that moment, and Atia had lost it. He immediately lost consciousness.

T Ⅲ ♯ T

Atia came back to awareness with a jerk. He had a terrible feeling of vertigo, an awful feeling of being held upside down. That feeling canceled out the awareness of a roadmap of aches and pains that were running along his slammed-down back running all the way to his chin.

Atia found himself hanging high in the air. By turning his head slightly, he could see for a great distance down, straight down.

He felt a set of powerful clamps holding onto his body, his shoulder and thigh. When he turned to look at them, he saw that the clamps were a pair of hands. Twisting his neck ever farther, he saw that they were the general's hands and that he was holding him at full arm's length above his head.

This was one very strong and powerful man.

The general stood at the very edge of the dropoff from the area where they had been fighting. Looking down Atia could not see where the bottom was. The drop that he was staring at had to be at least several hundred feet.

If the general were to let go of him, Atia thought that his body would add to the bird droppings smearing the cliff face on the way down. The rest of him would come to resemble washed-up jellyfish.

"Yes, look down, Atia," he said as he felt Atia stirring about. "All I have to do is to open up my hands and you are gone."

"I hear you," Atia said softly as he tried to figure out a way to drag the general with him if he were let go.

"I am not as clever a man as you," he said. "But I do have this one clear thought that you, Atia, had something to do with my brother Dal's death, and yet I can't prove it one way or the other."

"Look down one last time, Atia. Look down at the death I promise you if ever I find out that I was right about you and Dal."

"I give you back your life right now, but remember...."

He left his last word hanging out there as he turned back from the edge and threw Atia to the ground.

While he lay there groaning, the general turned and took his cape and sword. He mounted his horse and slowly continued down the same trail they had been traveling leading to the valley that the general had wanted to see.

The strange thing was that he knew that Atia would get up and follow him.

And he was right.

# CHAPTER TWENTY-NINE

**M**og had a problem, and he knew that he had to have the help of Kat, his human female slave, once again.

He was not happy knowing that there was no other Neanderthal that he could sit down with to work out a plan for the complete elimination of his human enemies.

It seemed that he, himself, was the only thinking Neanderthal in the entire army.

How was it that he alone could see and identify a problem when he saw one, try to figure out how to deal with it and then solve it? He acknowledged that it was true that his working staff could follow orders in great detail, and they would do everything that was asked of them, but not one of them could come up with a new and original idea. Everything that the Neanderthal soldiers did in a field fight was based upon whatever they had done before. They seemed to be unable to adapt themselves to changes of any kind.

Now that he was the Supreme Leader, and he had to answer to no one, he found himself alone, with no other army person to talk to about different situations. It bothered him that there was not one single Neanderthal out of their huge population that was a free thinker. He could not find one single first-rate intelligent mind within his entire military organization on whom he could count.

All roads seemed to lead back to Kat and her superior human brain. She had been very important in helping him plot how to get rid of the army officers who were ahead of him, and for that he was grateful. He was also grateful for the great sex that she gave him whenever and wherever the mood came upon him.

The truth of the matter was that no matter how many times he tried using his Neanderthal advisors, it was always to Kat that he would turn for advice, original thoughts and strategy. It was Kat who told him that he could not fight against an enemy and win if he did not know their strengths and weaknesses. Mog knew that she was right.

If he sent his Neanderthals into a direct battle with the humans, who now seemed to be working out new battle formations, he knew that the result would be the slaughter of his rough-and-tumble Neanderthals. They fought as individuals and not as trained and organized soldiers.

It was Kat who suggested that the two of them hide themselves somewhere near where the enemy was training, and watch and see what they were doing. It was Kat again who used his new favorite expression for the first time. She said that "knowledge of the enemy is the ability to defeat the enemy". He just loved this saying.

Mog had taken her advice, and the two of them had hidden themselves in the wooded area not far from where the humans were training.

Of course, in between watching the human soldiers, he had great sex with Kat right under the noses of the nearby sentries and all of the other humans. It was times like this that made life even more fun and exciting for them both.

When they were finally back to the safety of their own campgrounds, they talked about what they had just learned by watching all of the activities going on in and around the human camp. The most important issue that they both agreed upon was the fact that the humans had leaders that they called officers. These officers gave direct orders to the soldiers in the field. They were out there working with them until all the parts seemed to work together smoothly.

They both agreed that their original idea of creating human female officers was absolutely vital. They were amazed at how the human soldiers responded to the orders called out by their officers.

Kat also came up with another brilliant observation; one which Mog, himself, had completely missed. It appeared that the officers who were in the fields with the soldiers were called sergeants, and they took their orders from higher-up officers who were not out there with the fighting men. These absent officers were called captains. The captains were the ones who gave the orders to the sergeants, who then gave the orders to the soldiers who would be doing the fighting.

It also appeared that these captains got their orders from other higher-up officers who were called colonels and these colonels all reported to several generals. Finally all the generals took their orders from the one human that they called the Supreme Leader or Supreme Commander.

Kat said that she heard the name of the Supreme Commander Atia being spoken many times, and it was her conclusion that he was the head of the entire human army.

She said to Mog that there was another old human saying that she liked very much, and it was one that seemed to fit this situation perfectly. She said that the saying was "If you cut off the head, the body dies with it."

She said that if Mog were to have this Atia person killed just before one of the big battles that would be coming up soon, then the victory of the Neanderthals would be pretty much assured because each of the generals would want to replace the Supreme Leader and they would end up fighting among themselves. If they were having this inside fighting, how could they fight against the Neanderthals coming at them from the outside? The answer to the biggest of the problems facing them was to kill this Atia person just before one of the big battles.

*Remember, cut off the head and the body will die.*

Mog said that he would personally take on the responsibility of taking out this Supreme Leader Atia. He would do it himself so that there would be no screw-ups.

All he had to do was keep a secret watch on Atia to see where he went and what he did with his time. The trick was to get him alone; he would only need a few minutes with him. He should have no problem eliminating this one puny human who was standing in the way of his dominance of the entire world.

Mog was one happy Neanderthal as all of these ideas and all of the possibilities ran through his mind. He smiled at Kat as he repeated her earlier words with a slight change for his own enjoyment:

"When I cut off the head (Atia's), the body will die (the human soldiers)."

Mog smiled his huge Mog smile and quietly exited the tent.

# CHAPTER THIRTY

Atia, for the first time in many years, considered himself to be a happy man. His mate Ava and he were getting along well. He enjoyed spending whatever spare time he had with his soon-to-be-fifteen-year-old son Avoti, who was rapidly becoming a first-class hunter and fighting warrior.

At fifteen Avoti was still a year too young to do any actual fighting with the army, but he sat in on every military meeting. that Atia and his generals would have.

It was hoped that Avoti would become the tribe's leader one day and that listening to actual goings-on about the training and upcoming war would give him an understanding of the many things he would need to know if he were to become a leader in his own right.

Atia had made peace with General Ladd, which was very important to the war effort. Atia had arranged for the general and Ava to talk one evening. Their discussion had gone on from early evening until the first light of day the next morning. Ava gave him her first-hand, eyewitness account of how his brother Dal had actually died.

Ava must have been very convincing since the general had come to Atia and apologized deeply and meaningfully about the misunderstanding that they had had on the day they rode off together to look at the special valley the general had wanted Atia to see. They had cried together over the terrible death of Dal and, from that point on, General Ladd was his biggest supporter at the council meetings.

Atia was going over all of these things in his mind. He slowly walked along the flatlands where the human army was practicing for the soon-to-be-fought battle with the Neanderthals for the domination of the entire continent.

The Neanderthals were much more active now than they had ever been before. Humans could not travel about in small groups anymore without being attacked. The day-to-day gathering of fruits and vegetables from the outlying areas could only be done with heavily armed escorts.

For the past six months, reports of a new and more violent leader of the Neanderthals had been coming in to the general staff. It was reported that his name was Mog and that he also was preparing his people for the upcoming encounter between humans and Neanderthals.

The army of the humans was just about ready to be tested as the new and improved weapons were out there. All of the military tactics were being formulated every day.

What remained to be done was to pick a time and a place for a fixed battle and then force the Neanderthals to meet them on that battlefield.

The general staff had agreed that the best time was going to be in a few months from then when the weather would be going into early spring. The ground would then be dry and firm beneath the feet of the men and horses that they were hoping to put out there.

There was no doubt in Atia's mind that the humans would take the victory in the opening battle. It was the worldwide offensive plans against the Neanderthals that had him worried.

Mankind could not grow and prosper as long as any Neanderthals were still alive. This war had to be a war of complete extermination. To do this over the entire world was an almost-impossible undertaking.

Atia had walked as far as he wanted to go and was turning around to head back to camp when he saw a mounted figure bearing down on him from out of the cover of one of the nearby foothills. The rider was sitting astride a huge black and white horse that was pounding toward him at a very rapid pace.

Atia, who never panicked, quickly drew his sword. He noted that his assumed enemy already had his sword out and was waving it around his head as his great steed drew ever nearer to where Atia was standing.

Atia stood perfectly still and watched the waving sword very carefully noting that the rider was holding it in his left hand which would give Atia a slight advantage if he played out this scene carefully.

Everything was in the timing.

The horseman was perhaps a dozen yards away when Atia unexpectedly jumped across the path that it was taking toward him.

The rider was leaning downward on his left side to strike at what he saw as a right-handed opponent, when suddenly Atia was not there anymore. The horseman went on by where Atia had been standing only moments before.

As Atia leaped across the path of the oncoming mounted man and horse, he also swung his sword with all of his considerable strength behind it. It struck the rear leg of the horse as it pounded by. This sudden and, perhaps, cowardly blow to the leg of the horse caused it to fall onto its side. Fortunately for Atia it pinned its rider under its considerable weight.

It was only a few moments until Atia had disarmed the now helpless rider and put the poor horse out of its misery with a quick and lethal strike.

Atia had only a few seconds to decide what to do, and he thought it would be better to destroy the horse rather than let it suffer. He acted out of pure sympathy in the killing of the animal.

He then turned to see to the needs of the unconscious human rider who was lying there unmoving. Atia quickly tried to find a pulse in the neck of the rider but could not find any. The rider had broken his neck during the violent fall.

He then discovered that his attacker was not a man but a woman. This shocked him tremendously because he did not know that he had any female human enemies, let alone a female human enemy who had a war horse, a sword, and a reason to attack him.

Atia had no way of knowing at that particular moment that this brief fight based on the sudden attack against him would have world shaking after effects.

Lying there pinned under the dead horse was the female human slave to Mog known as Kat.

Kat, of course, was just a teenager and was impatient to move things along. She had kept her plans an absolute secret from Mog. She did not tell him what she was planning to do after she finished training with her recruited class of female human slaves.

She had practiced hard and long at becoming good at using a sword while on horseback.

She was looking forward to going back to Mog after she had taken care of the Atia person. It would be wonderful to tell him that she had personally taken care of the number-one enemy of the Neanderthals by herself.

She was sure that Mog would yell and scream and possibly even beat her, but that would not change the fact that she had solved his biggest problem.

The only thing that Kat did not take into consideration was the fact that Atia might not be so easily killed. It seemed to be so simple to overwhelm a single human male with a pounding horse and a swinging sword. She never thought about the possibility of putting herself in harm's way as a result of her own actions.

She had followed Atia's movements from a distance, and she knew where and when he would be taking one of his daily quiet walks.

Everything had gone perfectly as she came charging at Atia from her hiding place. She had her horse going at full speed in order to give Atia as little time as possible to react to her attack.

What she had not considered was that her limited personal experience with weapons and warriors had not prepared her to properly react to Atia's sudden jump to the side and his unexpected sideswipe at her horse.

She was not thinking about her own death, and how, if she died, Mog would be left without his best advisor just when he needed her most. Kat's only thought was for the glory that never came.

Atia did not know who Kat was and how important she was to the Neanderthal cause. To him she was just a rogue female human who must have been hired by the Neanderthals to kill him.

Hours later, when Atia reported his being attacked to the council, it was decided that the Neanderthals must have identified him as the human's Supreme Leader. It was further decided that he had to have personal protection whenever he left the compound. Over Atia's objections, the council posted their best security man to be with him and become his shadow.

᛭ �III ᚠ᛭

His name was X; simply X.

X would be with Atia exclusively for the protection and safety that he afforded.

He was endlessly patient, quiet and deadly. He was known to be tremendously fast in spite of his bulk, and he moved with a feline stealth that could explode into berserk action when needed.

X was the complete fighting machine, and he was to be Atia's insurance policy against any and all personal attempts on his life.

# CHAPTER THIRTY-ONE

Mog was in a rage after learning about Kat's stupidity. He knew that he had lost track of her yesterday, but that was not unusual. Kat would always wander around the compound, sometimes spending her time training with the other female humans or putting something together for Mog's meals.

He could not understand why she would do such a stupid thing. For a bright girl such a dumb thing was almost unbelievable. Nevertheless, what was done was done, and he could not get her back.

Mog had learned to always move on with things and, after he settled down a bit, he put together a plan of his own.

He knew that Atia would now always be protected whenever he went out of the campsite, and so he concluded that the best place to get at Atia was inside the human compound when no one would be guarding him.

He thought about whom to hire to do the job and concluded that there was no one better than himself. He knew that he could slip himself in and out of the human compound and find Atia easily enough.

Killing him would be no big deal, as he had killed the best of human warriors in hand-to-hand combats many times.

Now that he had a plan, he decided to let a few days go by so that things would calm down with the humans. He would go after this Atia person after he took himself on a little vacation.

Now that Kat was gone, there were two cute and well-put-together female slaves that he had his eye on. They would be perfect to help him relax. He would make the arrangements and have both of them sent up to his personal retreat in the mountains.

Sex always calmed him down, and doing it with two female human slaves would simply double his pleasure.

He spoke to his personal aide and told him who his choices were. He also instructed him to tell them both that, with Kat gone, he would be looking for one replacement slave to live with him.

If one or both of the girls really pleased him, then they would have a good idea from this first session of what making love to a real Neanderthal male was really like.

They did not know which of them he would pick to be his opening bed partner, so whoever was picked first would take the name of Number One.

The second girl whose job it was to finish off Mog's sexual dreams was to be known as Number Two.

Either one was quite prepared to be Number One or Two. It really did not matter, since they were both prepared to give the best sexual performance of their lives.

If they were a good team and could work well together, then Mog just might keep them both, and that would turn things around for the girls.

The way their lives were going as slaves, things were absolutely terrible, and they both knew that there was no other chance of escaping from their terrible lives except through Mog.

The time had arrived, and Mog finally appeared. He was dressed as if he were going to work with the troops.

The two girls simply smiled at him and completely ignored the way he was dressed.

They had a lot at stake here. This was Mog, and he was their lord and master.

Both girls were seventeen and had each matured quite well. Their bodies had well-rounded buttocks that were complemented by big breasts. The only real difference between the two of them was that one had light-colored hair and the other's hair was black in color.

"You, the dark one, what is your name?" he growled.

"I am called Number One, Sir Mog. Am I addressing you properly?"

"You may call me Mog, and you, the light-haired one, I assume you have the name of Number Two?"

"Yes, Mog. I am known as Number Two. If I might have your permission, I would like to mention a few things that Number One and I have been talking about. This conversation is all about you, Mog."

Mog sat down on the edge of the huge bed that dominated the large room. He was thinking that these two seemed well-meaning and quite spirited. They reminded him of the recently departed Kat.

He asked Number Two to tell him what they had on their minds.

"Mog," she said in a strong voice which did not let him know that she was quivering inside. "Number One and I are both seventeen years of age, and we both have been forced to sleep with many of your Neanderthal soldiers against our wills.

"Neither of us have found these to be good experiences because those males were just brutes who raped us and threw us out.

"We have obviously caught your attention or we would not be here now. We have noticed that we look pretty much alike, and it seems that you like what we look like because you requested both of us.

"We would like you to teach us what it is that you like in your bed and in your slaves, and we will perform these things to the best of our abilities.

"We are also smart. We can prepare your food and keep your clothes and room clean, and we can do all your chores.

"We are hoping that you will give us a chance to show you how good we can be. We know that between the two of us, we will absolutely exhaust you sexually each and every time you want to bed us down. We will consider this to be our jobs, and we will do it so well that you will never want any other females."

"And now, if I may be so bold, I would like to be the first to go to bed with you. If you would rather start with Number One and finish up with me, that will be fine."

For an answer, Mog stood up towering over the two of them. It was Number One that he put his mighty arm around and pulled close to him.

He was done with all the talking. He just wanted to screw.

It was only a matter of moments until Mog and Number One were completely undressed and standing there together, brushing their lips against each other in the first meaningful touch.

"Very nice and very distracting, Number One," he said as he pulled his head away from her kisses.

Number One forced herself to relax and give herself up to those delicious feelings that real sex was going to give her. She was worried that she might not enjoy having sex when she was not being raped.

She turned and planted baby kisses on his face. "Very inspiring," he said as he pressed his mouth against her well-developed right breast.

While he teased and sucked her breasts, she ran her hand down his back, raking it lightly with her fingernails.

His desire for her was already quite evident as she could feel it pressing against her thighs.

"Love me, Mog," she gasped hoarsely. "I'm ready for you."

"I will love you, Number One," he told her, raising his head to again gently kiss her lips. Then his mouth was on her, kissing her with a fierceness that was both surprising and thrilling to him. He was really enjoying himself.

While his tongue was darting in and out of her mouth, his hands found her buttocks and pressed them to his lower body.

Between the force of his powerful hands, and the hardness on the other side, she felt as if she were in a vise, caught between an irresistible force and the well -known immovable object.

She reached down as if to guide him into the place that was for him alone, but before she could manage it, he suddenly pulled away and turned her over onto her stomach.

With one hand cupping her breast, he lifted her torso easily with the other hand and entered her from behind. This seemed to be Mog's first choice of positions.

His large body was warming her back, his powerful knees were forcing open her thighs, and his teeth were nipping at her neck and ears. He moved with long, thrusting strokes, pinning her to the bed and using his body alone to do all the work.

The little moans of sexual pleasure that began to escape her lips were muffled by the pillow into which her face was being pressed.

Her breath came faster and faster as the thrusts came harder and harder. The sensations caused by this angle began to build up with an exquisite momentum for her.

She raised one of her arms high enough to touch his head with her hand, and she tugged at his soft hair like a drowning woman clutching a clump of seaweed.

She was absolutely mindless now, aware only of Mog's body atop hers, inside hers, stroking, thrusting. His movements were building up in speed as his own breath fell on her neck in hot rapid puffs.

Mog's exuberant cry of sexual release roared in her ears as his body collapsed against her back.

In a second or two more, her own release came, throbbing, exploding, and causing her to arch upward so that their union could not be destroyed.

"Mog. My god," she cried out, as simultaneously, they collapsed against each other, all the energy drained from both their bodies.

When she could speak again, her voice was a low rasp. "That was fantastic."

His mighty chest was still warming her backside as he lifted a strand of her hair from off of her forehead and kissed the back of her neck.

"You are fantastic, my love."

"I think I love you, Number One, and if Number Two is anything like you, I think we can all come to an understanding."

Number One knew that it was now time for her to leave the room. When it came to lovemaking, she always thought that the old saying of "two's a couple and three's a crowd" applied.

Just as the flap on the tent door closed with a loud swooshing sound, Number Two knew that it was her turn to take the center stage. She knew that she had Mog's attention as she paraded around the room wearing nothing but a great big smile.

Mog started to get up from the edge of the large bed and had not yet gotten his balance when all one hundred and fourteen pounds of her jumped into his startled arms.

They fell back onto the bed together, and it was only moments until she felt his warm lips move to the inside of her held wrists, up the sensitive part of her inner arm, and then over to the crook of her neck.

His warm tongue trailed languidly along her skin as he went to work on this willing female human.

In order to get this first trial going, she reached up and clasped herself to him, fastening her shapely breasts against his hairy chest and feeling the rise of his hardness against her thighs as he moved his body about.

He kissed her again on the mouth, hard, his strong tongue invading hers, filing up her mouth, only to withdraw and then flick inward again.

Her hands gripped his buttocks, kneading the rounded firmness, occasionally allowing her fingertips to dig in gently and waken him up fully to her sexual overtures.

She had never known a man, either human or Neanderthal, who within minutes of just completing his own sexual moments could ready himself for a second round. This Neanderthal was an amazing bed partner, and she began to understand why he was looking for two women instead of the usual one.

She reached for his hardness, running her fingertips over the sensitive places and thrilling to the realization that he was ready for her as she was for him.

Feeling Number Two's tantalizing manipulations, Mog began to groan and mutter something in a language she didn't understand.

Suddenly he pulled up and reached for her breasts again, handling them firmly, drawing first one and then the other into his mouth, teasing her nipples with his tongue, and causing her body to arch upward on its own in what was beginning to be mindless rapture for her.

And then her breasts were freed, and he was moving downward, grasping her thighs and lifting her upward, while his head plunged toward the curling mound of softness that called him.

As Number Two gasped and writhed in a frenzy of desire, his tongue flicked and darted as it had done in her mouth, only this time it was bouncing off places that caused her senses to spiral upward. She felt as if she were in the eye of a turbulent yet exquisite storm.

"Mog, you're driving me crazy. Stop your teasing and let me feel you inside me. I want you now, and I want all of you. Please Mog, do it now."

He entered her; his strokes were slow at first, but then they came faster and harder.

Number Two could feel herself an instant away from the blazing climax she was now craving, and yet she forced herself to hold back. But her resolve was getting weaker as her insides were turning to jelly and the dam was about to be opened. There was nothing she could do about it.

Then she heard Mog's cry, felt his stiffening, and she too cried out as she felt herself arching toward him.

They clasped each other in an almost desperate embrace as they reared and bucked and rolled together until they were both gasping for breath, no longer capable of movement of any kind.

Absolute stillness pervaded the large bedroom as the fireplace crackled and offered them its comforting warmth.

It was Mog who got up first and got dressed in silence.

It was Mog who walked out the door and closed it quietly so as not to disturb the now-sleeping human female.

It was Mog who walked a little ways, looked up at the stars in the sky and thought *this is a wonderful world and soon it will be all mine.*

# CHAPTER THIRTY-TWO

everal weeks had gone by since the attack on Atia by Kat on horseback. The human compound was now on special alert at all times.

It was now believed that the Neanderthals would try to eliminate the generals and the Supreme Leader if they could.

It was X's job, as the new chief of security, to keep the compound under tight control and keep everyone within it safe from outsiders.

Atia was content just standing there and watching the busy goings on around him as the compound's people went about their daily business.

The human council had put out the official word that there soon would be an organized all-out attack on the Neanderthals.

Almost every human in the entire compound had lost a friend or loved one to an attack from the Neanderthals. When the call for soldiers went out, male humans by the hundreds were volunteering to train and to fight with the newly united armed forces. The motivation was, basically, revenge, and fear for their loved ones if they did nothing to stop these hated enemies.

Human manpower was no longer the problem it used to be. Everyone was now aware that unless the Neanderthal problem was solved once and for all, the future did not look good for the entire human race. They flocked to the army, both the young males and many older men, who all feared going up against the Neanderthals but feared more what would happen if they did not stand and fight for themselves. Their loved ones and the future of the human race were at stake.

And now that the problem of getting enough human fighters was solved, the new and most important problem was one of getting them properly trained and having enough weapons for everyone.

Weapons of the old kind and weapons of the new kind were now in high production, but still the time factor was not in favor of the humans. Making the spear thrower and longbow were items that had to be done by hand and the number of skilled weapons' makers was limited.

Atia took one last look around the area and noted that the posted guards were in place before he stepped into his personal field office/sleeping tent. He had a full day tomorrow, and he knew that he needed to get a good night's sleep.

His tent was a little bit off from the usual path that everyone used. This was done in order to give him a bit of privacy and to allow him to hold meetings where outsiders would not be listening.

From the very moment that he stepped through the entrance of his tent and ducked through the doorway into the shadowy interior of the large single room, Atia immediately sensed that someone else was already inside. The night sky was just beginning to darken, but the ventilation cuts made into the canvas walls let in enough light by which to see.

The usual fire that was always burning in the corner fireplace was out, and no candles were burning at all.

Atia felt a presence in the inky shadows of the tent. He felt something dark and menacing, and he definitely could hear someone breathing slowly and deeply.

Something moved slightly in the darkest corner of the room. Atia went to his holding belt and pulled out the twelve-inch knife that he always carried with him whenever he left his tent.

172

He pulled the knife in front of him and stood very still with all of his senses on alert. He thought to himself that pulling his knife was probably a silly and useless gesture if the person in the room turned out to be the one he thought it was.

If he were going to die, then he wanted to give a good accounting of himself, and so he stood there with his long knife in his hand.

"Mog," he whispered. "Is that you?"

"Yes, Atia, I am Mog. You should have expected me to make this visit to you, Atia. If our positions were reversed, you would have been looking for me.

Without you being there on the battlefield when our armies meet, Human Supreme Leader Atia, my Neanderthals will have a better chance.

"I admire you as a wartime leader, Atia, and by watching what you have been doing, I have improved my own army. You are an interesting human, and I am truly sorry that you soon will die at my hand."

Mog's harsh rough voice sent a chill along Atia's spine as he tried to make out his bulky form, which was mostly hidden in the deep shadows cast inside the room.

"You are a fool, Atia, to try to match your humans against my Neanderthals in a fair fight. The truth is that we don't really know how to fight fair. We only know how to fight to win. Without you out there, my victory is almost a sure thing."

"After our upcoming head-to-head fight, you humans will be in full retreat here and around the rest of the world. Soon there will be no humans left, and then the entire continent will be left to my Neanderthal people. That is my goal, and that is my plan."

"But now I grow tired of all this talk, Atia. It is time for us to settle this once and for all."

The shadows exploded as Mog's vast bulk suddenly leaped at Atia, and the two of them smashed against the thin walls of the tent.

The force of the two of them tore right through the wall material, and they tumbled to the ground outside and onto the flat and open surface surrounding the isolated structure.

At least now Atia could see clearly. He could see the great, hulking Neanderthal, and Mog could see him.

It was Atia's only hope that the guards, who were off in the distance, would see and hear them fighting and come running to his aid. One on one against Mog, he knew that he did not stand a chance.

Mog's powerful fingers were now reaching for his throat as Atia slashed wildly at him with his knife, but it was no use to him at all. He saw Mog's face only inches away from his own face as Atia's knife was knocked out of his hand.

Mog had a wide leering grin on his evil face that pulled his ugly teeth to the forefront, and they gleamed wickedly at Atia.

A brutal snarl growled up from Mog's throat as his eyes began blazing with his triumphant fury.

The strength was rapidly seeping out of Atia's muscles and his attempts to fight off Mog began to fail. Darkness started to cloud over his vision, and Atia knew that he was about to die.

Then suddenly something thudded into the massive body of Atia's attacker, and Mog suddenly released his grip on Atia. He whirled about to see from where the spear had come.

As he gratefully let the ever-so- precious air into his starving lungs, Atia saw that Mog was standing above him with a long spear dangling from his side. Blood oozed from the wound as Mog turned and snarled his defiance.

In the distance, Atia saw X release another spear in their direction. This time Mog caught it with one hand and threw it back at one of the guards who was running rapidly at them.

It was an alert X who had quickly thrown that first spear and absolutely saved Atia's life. Another few seconds and it would have been all over for Atia.

As he was making his rounds, X saw the two bodies crash

through the tent and had immediately recognized the danger to Atia. His quick reaction was the difference between life and death for Atia.

As Mog turned to face the rapidly approaching guards, spears began to fall all around him. While Mog's attention was off him, Atia was able to kick at his legs, which caused Mog to almost fall over as he sought to regain his balance.

Mog snarled at Atia as he pulled the long spear out of his side and threw it at Atia. Atia was smart enough to jump behind the thick wooden table that was lying on its side where it had crashed through the tent wall with the struggling men.

Even with the awkward off-balance throw of the spear at Atia, the strength behind Mog's· throw allowed the spear to completely penetrate the thick wooden table where it barely missed the crouched Atia.

Mog turned and, with surprising quickness in someone so big, lumbered off toward the nearby hills.

The flow of blood coming from his side did not slow Mog down for a moment as X and the guards finally got to Atia, who was sitting on the ground.

None of the guards were brave or stupid enough to chase after the lumbering giant who was just entering the first of the low foothills.

It was only minutes later that his mate, Ava, arrived with more guards. She hugged Atia, making a fuss over him.

She quickly applied healing leaves to his throat, where she had noticed the large fingerprints that Mog's fingers had left there. She knew that Atia was lucky to be alive.

"Who was that?" one of the guards asked.

Now standing with the help of Ava and one of the guards, Atia replied in a soft voice that carried among all the gathered people, "That was the enemy of all men. That was our enemy whose only desire is to kill us all.

"That was Mog!"

# CHAPTER THIRTY-THREE

Avoti, son of Atia and Ava, was not a happy young man. Here he was, almost seventeen years old, and he had nothing to do with himself. He was simply bored.

They told him that he was too young to train with the newly formed army (he had to be seventeen), too young to offer advice at the council meeting where his father always brought him to sit and listen, and too young to do anything that he thought was important for the good of the tribe. So he did the next best thing for a young and physically mature young man to do; he decided to go hunting.

He thought about asking one or more of his friends to join him but thought better of it. They would probably want to go somewhere different from where he wanted to go.

Avoti just wanted to get out there into the wild and get away from constantly thinking about how close his father had come to being killed.

He was told that it would be a few weeks until Atia would be up and about, and a hunting trip for himself seemed to make a lot of sense.

He only took the basic essentials with him: flint for fire, something for his food, his new longbow with many extra arrows, and finally his highly prized twin set of hunting knives that his mother and father had given him on his sixteenth birthday. The hunting knives were the most exciting gifts that he had ever received.

Atia himself had cast them in the hottest fires and molded them until they were perfectly balanced. Avoti

had spent weeks practicing with them until he could hit his intended target while on his feet or lying down or hiding behind a tree.

He was so good with them now that he did not even have to think about the act of knife-throwing, he would just have to make the moves and the knife never missed its intended target.

He carried the knives on his body in exactly the same way that the human soldiers did. One was in a wraparound leg holder, and the other was in a special pull-and-throw holder that he wore attached to his working belt. He was never without both knives attached to his body. This was something that was drilled into his head by Atia, who always said that a pair sent the message loud and clear.

He even learned to sleep in such a position that the knives that slept with him were not uncomfortable at his side.

After spending the early hours of the morning visiting with his father, he gave his goodbyes to his mother and a few friends and headed off by himself into what the tribes called "the wilderness".

His world, during the Ice Age, had its glittering glaciers, beautifully clear rivers, thundering waterfalls, and hordes of wild animals.

The vast grasslands that seemed to go on and on forever were dramatically dangerous to the unwary traveler, and were most brutally harsh.

Avoti and his people, who lived there, recognized at a very fundamental level that this was their world, and it was theirs to shape.

As he left the settlement behind him, he set a slow and leisurely pace for himself. He wanted to learn about the land he was about to make his own.

Avoti noted that layers of glacial ice melted at various depths depending on their local conditions. In the cool and shaded areas with heavy moss or other insulated vegetation, the ground melted only a few inches. But where the land was exposed to direct sunlight, it softened more, and this softening allowed an abundant grass cover to grow. The grass was what attracted all of the animals who lived in the wild. The humans and Neanderthals always followed the animals because they were one of the main sources of food and clothing for them.

For the most part Avoti noted that local weather conditions did not favor the growth of large trees with their deeper root systems. In places that were protected from the coldest winds and the hardest frosts, several feet of topsoil usually thawed enough for local trees to take root.

The Bronze Age human beings always settled wherever an abundance of fruit-bearing trees and brush were to be found. These trees were also an amazingly rich resource that provided a wealth of materials, especially firewood, for those who lived near enough to the forests.

The gathering of fruits and vegetables, along with the hunting of small animals, was always the job for the women of the tribe. Hunting of the larger animals was always given to the men who were the gatherers of large food and game for the tribe.

Avoti walked on his way along the path between the clear sparkling water of the local river and the black -streaked white limestone cliffs. He followed the trail as far as it went. It was leading him away from the outskirts of his settlement encampment.

The sun was still low in the eastern sky, but a brilliant band of red, fading to purple at the edges, announced the arrival of the corning day. A tinge of pink highlighted the thin nebulous bank of stratus clouds on the western horizon reflecting the back side of the glowing sunrise.

After about a fifteen-minute walk, he found the ground starting to angle downward at a fairly steep angle. It was a most unusual configuration of the land in that off to the side he could see a natural formation of a long, wide and shallow-looking ramp that angled downward into a fairly deep open pit.

No bird sounds were heard in the distance, though birds normally sang unless something or someone startled them into silence.

Above the new area where he was now beginning to walk, even the ever-present vultures could find no upward-lifting air currents upon which to soar in their continuous, never-ending search for food.

The icy air hung deadly still as Avoti carefully looked around.

He was curious about the strange-looking down ramp that led into the pit, and he walked over to one of the sides. He looked down but did not see anything at all that seemed to be out of place.

Most of the large area was still cast in semidarkness as the rising sun cast shadows into the pit.

A slight drizzle had fallen and at the bottom of the ramp, the softer earth had turned slightly muddy.

Seeing nothing that seemed to be a threat to him, Avoti slowly walked down the sloping and irregular ramp until he reached the flat bottom of the pit.

He was getting a weird feeling about this place, and he decided to head back up the ramp but, before he did so, he put his hand on the tied-down belt-holding pouch that held the first of his two knives. He took a firm hold on the blade's handle but did not draw out the knife. Just holding his hand on the handle of the weapon gave him some of the comfort that a weapon always afforded him.

As he dropped down to one knee to make himself a smaller target in case someone was watching him, he heard a high-pitched war cry coming from about halfway up the ramp which was now behind and slightly above him.

Suddenly something slammed into his back with such a great amount of force that Avoti was driven face first into the slightly wet ground. He had to lie there for a few moments in order to recover the breath that had been knocked out of him.

Finally, he came back to his senses and jumped to his feet. He probably should have waited a bit longer, because as he stood up, he realized that he was still dizzy and somewhat wobbly on his feet.

As he caught his breath and tried to get his bearings, he saw someone standing about ten feet away from him. He was breathing deeply to get his wind back while he stared at his new enemy, which had just announced its arrival in a very big way.

Avoti stood there and looked at a young and not very big Neanderthal warrior, who was holding and pointing a huge spear in his right hand.

He appeared to be young to Avoti, but it was hard for Avoti to judge because of his lack of experience with Neanderthals.

Avoti was able to tell that they were both about the same five foot in height, but the young Neanderthal was about twice his width. Avoti, who weighed in at about a slim one hundred thirty pounds, thought that he was looking at about a one-hundred-seventy-pound brute. Besides the weight advantage that would give it more strength than Avoti, the Neanderthal was holding a huge two-sided spear that he moved back and forth from his left hand to his right, which seemed to be his more natural hand.

The Neanderthal had a spear and Avoti only had a knife. He realized that he was at a great disadvantage as to weapon and body strength.

Avoti now knew who it was that was trailing him, and he realized that he was in big trouble with no one else around to help him. He had to help himself if he wanted to live.

Finally, the Neanderthal broke the silence. "So we meet at last, Son of Atia." He smiled the usual ugly Neanderthal smile.

Avoti was happy just to stand there quietly for a few moments as he still needed time to recover from unexpectedly getting knocked down.

The Neanderthal seemed to want to talk, and that was fine with Avoti, as he waited for his head to clear.

Putting an equally big smile on his face, Avoti replied in a soft voice, "Screw you, big guy."

He was surprised that he got no reaction from the Neanderthal. It showed neither anger nor amusement at his comments.

"I want you to know, son of Atia, that another human once said that to me, and he is no longer among the living. That is just the way you will be in a few minutes."

"The son of the famous leader Atia will be quite a trophy for me to take back to leader Mog. There is a big reward out for any of you humans, and a family member like you will double my riches."

Avoti felt a great anger rising inside him, but he knew that he had to keep it under control if he wanted to walk away from all of this.

The Neanderthal was speaking, "I know that you are alone, son of Atia, and I want you to know that I, too, am alone. This fight will be between the two of us."

"My name is Krull. There is no one here to help either one of us. This was meant to be, now that we know each other by name."

He continued, "It is your fate to be here with me, and my fate to cut off your face."

Avoti assumed that Krull had brought his own knife along for what he had in mind, and he said to him, "You are welcome to try for my face, Krull, but it will be kind of hard for you to do that with your spear. Why don't we see who the better man is and go at it with just knife against knife?

Your knife against my knife will be the true measure of who we are, that is unless you are afraid to meet me now with equal weapons."

"I will not kill you quickly, son of Atia, unless you force me to. I want to drag out your agony.

I want to cut off your balls, and then slowly slice off your face, as I just said."

Avoti had no reply to that, so he just kept silent and let him rant and rave.

Krull reached behind his back and produced a long and very wide knife.

He said, "This is what I will use. You will still be alive to feel it and to feel your face being pulled from your skull."

Avoti thought to himself that he had to stop seeing these sick types of enemies. He laughed to himself at his own sense of humor.

Krull completely surprised Avoti by throwing his spear away from him and off to the side. This was much more to Avoti's liking. Even though the Neanderthal still had the advantage in size and strength, knife to knife rather than knife against spear gave him a better chance.

Avoti stood there and looked at Krull very carefully, with his huge body, ugly face, and one very large and dangerous-looking knife.

Krull stood perfectly still, looking right back at Avoti. His legs were slightly apart and bent at the knees, and his muscular arms were away from his sides.

Krull had gone into a classic knife-fighting position and that told Avoti that he either was well taught or had beaten someone who had used that stance but lost the fight anyway.

But anything could happen in a one-on-one knife fight.

# CHAPTER THIRTY-FOUR

Krull began to move from left to right, and Avoti shifted himself to match directions. Krull then stopped circling and slowly moved toward his enemy saying, "I once flayed a human's flesh from his chest. I could see his ribs, his lungs and his beating heart."

He came closer, and Avoti could see his face more clearly in the dim light. He looked just like the rest of the Neanderthals. He had the deep, dark and narrow-set eyes separated by that flat nose, giving him a monkey-like appearance. It was not a good-looking face.

He kept coming closer, brandishing his long knife at Avoti with a big smile on his ugly face. Avoti stepped back, and Krull smiled wider. He was really having fun.

He moved closer, slicing the air with his blade. Avoti continued to step back, and again Krull closed the gap between them.

Krull flipped his knife into the air, then caught it by its handle and smiled at Avoti as he showed off his skill. While his attention was on the toss and catch of his weapon, Avoti carefully drew his blade from its holder at his waist.

Avoti's knife was about half the length of the Neanderthal's, but he was now armed and hopefully just as dangerous.

Avoti turned, took a step backward, pretended to slip in the mud, and then suddenly spun around on his knees, letting Krull run straight into the extended knife, which caught him in his groin.

Krull let out a surprised scream and backpedaled away from Avoti. Avoti stood up and charged for the kill before Krull could recover from the shock of the blade to his personal parts.

Krull knew that he was badly hurt. He held his knife hand over his bleeding groin area while his other hand began feeling around for the spear that he had thrown down.

As he was backing up and away from Avoti, he stepped onto the long spear handle and lost his balance, falling backward into the mud.

The only move that Avoti had was to dive onto Krull in order to keep that deadly spear out of his hands. While he was doing that, Avoti was watching for the long knife that Krull was still holding.

Avoti saw that Krull was beginning to bleed out, but with his superior size and strength, Avoti could not count on his weakening any time soon.

Avoti made a running jump and landed fully on Krull's chest. Avoti's timing was just right. Krull was starting to raise his legs to catapult him into the air and away from him.

His normally slow Neanderthal moves were even slower now that Avoti had given him a rapidly bleeding wound, and so Avoti was able to avoid Krull's attempt to hurl him away.

Krull's arm was rushing for a stab at him, but Avoti was much faster than the Neanderthal, and besides that he was uninjured.

Avoti was able to grab Krull's thick wrist and hold on to it as he kept the weight of his body on Krull. Krull struggled to get Avoti off of him and to get his knife hand away. He got a tight grip on Avoti's wrist while he lifted his head. His strong teeth bit down hard on Avoti's cheek.

The bite sent flashes of pain through Avoti's head, but he never let go of Krull's knife hand.

Even though he was still holding onto Krull's wrist, Avoti managed to get his arm up, and he brought the butt end of his knife handle down on the top of Krull's head.

Krull released his bite on Avoti's cheek. Avoti twisted his hand just enough to bring the sharp end of his blade to inches above Krull's forehead.

If Avoti could have finished the move, it would have ended the fight, but Kru11 was incredibly strong, and he held Avoti's swinging arm at a standstill as they grasped each other. They were suddenly locked together, neither of them able to use their knives or let go of the grip they had on each other. This could go on until one of them weakened or did something unexpected or desperate. Krull was in very good physical condition, and he did not seem to be tiring as Avoti knew that he would be soon.

The blood, which was still flowing from Krull's groin injury, was not helping Avoti as much as he had hoped that it would, while they each continued to try to break free from each other's grip.

Krull kept trying to get his knee into Avoti's groin, but he had no leverage, and the human kept his full weight on him. He tried to get his teeth into Avoti's face again, but Avoti kept his head tilted back until Krull gave up on that idea.

Avoti had no idea where exactly he had struck him: his genitals? his thigh? his lower stomach? It didn't seem to matter where the wound was. It was not bleeding fast enough to be of any real help to Avoti.

They made eye contact and stared at each other. Avoti said to the Neanderthal, "You are going to die, Krull, and the great Mog will never know what happened to you."

Krull shook his large head and said, "You" His voice was still very deep.

As they continued to struggle, Avoti realized that Krull was not weakening at all, but he was. Krull knew it and was waiting Avoti out. It was time for the human to do something desperate. He gave him a head butt, but it didn't cause him any more pain than it did Avoti.

Avoti then clamped his teeth on Krull ' s nose, and bit down as hard as he had ever bitten on anything. Before Krull screamed, Avoti felt the blood oozing out of his nose and into Avoti's mouth.

Krull was in real pain now, so he barely noticed that Avoti had released his bite on his nose to spit blood into Krull's left eye. When that eyelid automatically closed, Avoti got his teeth on it and ripped the area around his eye and then spit more blood into that eye.

A man, whether human or Neanderthal, when in great pain, will suddenly develop super-strength as the body of adrenaline charges his muscle power for several moments.

The young Neanderthal had the rush of adrenaline as he reared up and threw Avoti completely off him.

It took Avoti a few moments to regain his balance as he slowly began to rise, but those few seconds were all that he needed. He was ready to finish this off.

Both Avoti's hands were free now, and he pulled Krull's head back by his long hair and slashed his throat. Avoti then pushed him face down into the mud where he belonged.

Avoti stood there absolutely motionless as he watched the dark mud tum red with the blood that had rushed out of Krull's body.

There was no doubt that he was dead, and that was a good thing, because Avoti's head was spinning. He was so dizzy that he could barely stand.

Avoti walked a good ten feet away and sat down on the ramp. He stared up at the sky and felt a light drizzle of rain coming down along with the sunshine.

It felt wonderful just being alive. He lost control of himself and began to laugh and laugh. He couldn't stop for many minutes. This was his first one-on-one fight with an enemy and, even though he was battered, bitten and aching all over, he had survived and won.

What a great feeling it was to be alive.

He walked over to the farthest corner away from the body of his dead enemy and instantly began falling asleep. He knew that he needed to sleep and then retrace his steps back home to the settlement where he could get some attention to all his bodily problems.

His body was sore but his mind was soaring with the eagles. He had met the enemy face to face and had defeated him man to man.

Complete darkness overtook his mind as he fell into the deepest of sleeps.

# CHAPTER THIRTY-FIVE

Zane smelled good to Avoti, and he thought that she looked even better. It was a semi-sweet exotic and tingling sensation of a smell that pleased him very much.

He thought of Zane as if she were one of those special flowers that he had seen on his many wanderings in the forest surrounding the human settlement. She was like that very special flower that blooms wonderfully in the sunshine but saves its best for the dark shades of night.

Avoti and Zane had quietly left the meeting hall where his father Atia had called for an emergency council meeting to talk about the aggressive actions being taken by the Neanderthals. Everyone was very nervous about how close to the settlement Avoti had been attacked, and the settlement was put on high alert until certain decisions had been made.

Avoti told Zane that his father was going to push for a punishing attack against the Neanderthals by the foot and horse soldiers who were nearly ready for their first fight on the battlefield.

Atia had told him that even though the human fighters were just about ready to test themselves against the enemy, they had to be very careful about how the first encounter took place. He wanted to pick the battlefield area and prepare things so that the advantage would be with the human forces.

The council had to make sure that the first encounter was a successful one. If the first fight against the Neanderthals was not a great success, then all of their other plans would fall apart. They needed an absolute victory and nothing less. That was what they would be talking about at the latest meeting.

Avoti had been the first to testify about his personal encounter with the young Neanderthal who was hanging around the surrounding forests of their settlement. He told them that he was told that Mog, their new leader, had put a price on the head of any and every human. Avoti was sure that the enemy he had fought with was only the beginning and that other Neanderthals would be coming around looking for a fight.

After his testimony he took his father's hug and met Zane, who was waiting for him outside.

As the guards surrounding the special meeting hall were getting set up, Avoti led Zane away from there with the destination in mind of going to the now -empty hut where his father was attacked and almost killed by Mog.

The two teenagers, Avoti, almost seventeen, and Zane, almost thirteen, were fully mature physically as was the norm for Bronze Age young humans.

Females obtained their full growth around their thirteenth birthdays and had an average lifespan possibly into their late forties. Males matured a bit later and were not considered fully grown until they were sixteen or seventeen years old. The average lifespan for males and females was based upon their avoiding diseases, wild animal attacks, food poisoning, Neanderthal attacks, etc.

These two teenagers could hardly wait to be alone with each other. They had been seeing each other only at all the social gatherings of the tribe, but never had they been alone as they now found themselves.

It was easy for Avoti to put the near-death experience out of his mind as he looked at the beautiful Zane.

Slowly he slid his fingers under her chin, moving inch by inch toward her right ear. Avoti was taking great personal pleasure in this first and most important contact with her skin. The very texture of her was smooth and velvety as it had looked to him, and he felt the fire and heat coming from her closely-pressed body.

He sensed, in a deep down and very primitive way, the simmering heat of her needs along with his own.

He touched her earring, which was a simple carved-bone hoop, and then caressed her earlobe tucking back her long black hair.

Like a smoothly moving cat, she turned her cheek into his moving fingers. Leaning down from his height of an even five feet, he kissed her lightly with a brief brush against her lips. Avoti only wanted the slightest taste of her in this first brief exchange of a kiss.

"I would like another kiss," she said quietly. "A real kiss this time because I want to know if it will be as good as I am thinking it will be." He was still smiling as he leaned toward her again and held her, gently giving her what she wanted.

Their lips were parted, and tongue met tongue.

Avoti had kissed many girls in his first seventeen years of life, but this first real kiss completely shut out the world for him. Suddenly the world around him was gone. It was just him, the beautiful Zane and that wonderful kiss that existed.

He knew that there was something special going on here, and he wanted to explore these sensations to the fullest. He closed his eyes as he kissed her again to better savor the taste of her. She tasted of sweet meats and sugar.

He forgot about going slowly. He forgot about deliberation and restraint.

He pulled her closely against him, crushing her soft and female form up against himself. His other hand slid beneath the nape of her neck to hold her in place. He bent her slightly backward, holding her slight weight against him, and experienced who she was physically through her soft and giving body which she pressed tightly up against his. He continued to smell that special smell of hers that seemed to be inside of his pounding head.

The age-old primitive man part of him fought for dominance within him. The instinct that ancient man had passed down to this modern Bronze Age youth had, for generations beyond counting, told him to rip her clothes off and take her right there and then. But a lifetime of civilized ways taught to him by Atia and Ava, his honored parents, quickly overruled the lust that now was thundering through his young body.

Stepping back to allow some time and space between them, he quickly removed his outer clothing and put his arms around her yielding waist.

Another single kiss from Avoti to Zane was like dying and being reborn in the heady space of a second.

For one moment Zane was full of doubt and antagonism, and the next she was being seduced by the instant flow of response and the emotional intensity of her mood.

Her skin felt cold and clammy to her, but her mouth was on fire beneath his. Her nerve endings were tingling as he pried her lips apart and plunged his tongue into the tender interior of her waiting mouth. It was passion at its most primal level, as the naked flood of chemical reactions smashed down all her resistance to his aggressive behavior.

Her head swam, her legs trembled violently, and her hands clutched him in order to steady herself.

His breath mingled with hers, sweet, so sweet. It was an unbearable aphrodisiac, and her fingers rose to spear into his thick black hair, holding him to her while trading kiss for passionate kiss. She reveled in the pressure of his warm and sensual mouth on hers.

The width of his muscular chest crushed the swollen contours of her breasts as she pushed herself against him, defenseless in the grip of her overriding need to get even closer to him.

His hand spread across her buttocks and urged her into more intimate contact. She rocked against him, thrilled by the long hard ridge of his arousal.

With a guttural groan, he shifted even closer inviting her touch, while he bent down and used his gentle hands to quickly remove her clothing.

His long, sure fingers trailed up over the exposed length of her thighs until she shivered and shook with longing.

The heat at the heart of her was more than she could withstand, and her thighs pressed together tightly as if to seal in the ache of need before easing apart again.

She shivered as he found her most sensitive spot with his skilled insistence. He rubbed the tiny bud, and she moaned out loud, quivering in his hold like an eager racehorse at the starting line, out of breath, and empty of any thoughts, fully possessed by her sudden hunger.

A choked cry escaped her as he explored the swollen silky flesh between her thighs. Then he dropped down to his knees and used his mouth and his tongue on the tender tissue.

Beneath that sensual onslaught, Zane's legs shook like mad.

His arms held her steadily when all control was wrested from her by her enthralled response to his exquisite carnal expertise.

Her body was on the very edge, surging and hurtling toward orgasm, when he suddenly sprang upright and lifted her off of her feet.

He brought her bottom down on the recently unused soft grass mat that had belonged to his father. His father was far from his mind as his impatient hands basely parted her thighs.

He slid into her, long and impossibly thick and hard, stretching her honeyed channel to capacity. As he withdrew and then slammed back into her swollen softness, the delirious excitement washed back upon her in an intoxicating tidal wave of feelings.

With each one of his bold strokes, erotic ripples of pleasure assailed her. He held her tightly to him while his hands held her hips firmly. He thrust more deeply into her with highly rhythmic movements.

Zane was completely out of control and out of her mind with excitement.

When he drove her into a climax, she screamed in release, shuttering and shaking from the seething intensity of sensations that threatened to tear her body apart as she traveled from the height of stressed-out tension to ecstatic limpness.

As if from a distance, she heard his voice speaking to her. "You are the most incredibly sexy female I've ever met."

"I love you, Zane." Avoti stopped speaking. He spread a string of tender kisses across her freckled nose.

It was only moments later that the two young lovers were in each other's arms, soundly sleeping.

# CHAPTER THIRTY-SIX

Mog had several problems with no solutions in sight. He had an army of over three thousand Neanderthals who were well armed, well trained and who were looking forward to doing battle with the humans.

The issue with the Neanderthal army was the same one that had held the Neanderthals back from world domination for generations. They were great fighters who were willing to die for Mog and the Neanderthal people. This was well and good, but Mog realized that if he sent them out in an open battle against the humans, they would be slaughtered.

The problem was a very straightforward one, and the solution seemed to be out of his control.

The humans were trained to fight as a team, and they responded well to orders given to them by other humans, whom they called officers. There was little doubt that the human soldiers would do well under battle conditions.

His Neanderthals, if they could only battle the humans in a one-on-one personal fight, would win nine out of ten of those fights. But it didn't work that way. The humans fought as a team and his Neanderthals refused to do that.

No matter what he tried to do with his Neanderthals, they were not able to follow a fighting command from any of his own officers. He had used officers who knew each and every Neanderthal in their command on a personal basis. They knew each soldier by their first name, but it didn't seem to matter. They would not take orders from another Neanderthal when it came to fighting.

He tried making officers out of human slave girls who had shown him some abilities to lead, but his men simply ended up dragging the would-be officers into the nearest wooded area and sexually attacking them. Traditionally that was what they did with female slaves, and there was nothing he could do that would make them take their orders.

Another problem that Mog had with his armed forces was that humans had learned to tame and ride horses. A human on horseback, swinging a club or sword, was something to fear, and his soldiers had learned how to be afraid. Being afraid of puny humans had sent shivers down the backs of many of his men. When they would see a mounted human horse soldier coming at them, they almost always turned and ran.

The few brave or possibly stupid ones who didn't run from the horse soldiers did not live to tell him about it.

Mog had the original idea of putting his own men on horseback, but the horses would not let his men come close to them. He was told that it was a fear of the hunting Neanderthals that had been inbred into the wild horses and had taught them to escape. It was something in the body odor of the Neanderthals that drove horses wild and unusable. Too many centuries of hunting horses down for food could not be changed in time to take advantage of them as war horses.

When human horse soldiers would be taking the battlefield against his Neanderthals, Mog knew that the massive weight of the horse and human rider far outweighed his Neanderthals, and when they came charging across the field on horseback and waving their club or sword, it was almost impossible to order his men to stand

and take the charge. This put him at another disadvantage in this game of war.

He had been trying to probe the humans for weaknesses, so he sent out dozens of his smartest men to act as spies. Their assignment was not to engage or fight with the humans as they watched them train but to watch, learn, and then report their findings back to him.

Not one of his spies who might have gotten close to the training areas ever came back.

After his ill-fated personal attack on Atia inside the stockade, the humans had doubled and tripled their security. Mog, who was used to knowing everything
that the humans were doing, was now just guessing, and that was not the way he wanted to fight a war of extermination.

He had decided, therefore, to approach his problem in a simple, twofold manner. He would send his two new personal female human slaves to see Atia and his council and to ask if they would sit down to talk about a truce—something like dividing up the world into two equal parts might be acceptable to them all.

If that did not work, he would try to work out a plan where he could engage a small group of humans and put an overwhelming force of Neanderthals against them to see if the greater number of fighters on his side would make a difference. This would only act as a trial to see if changing his tactics would make a possible change in the upcoming human/Neanderthal war.

If he could win many small battles against the humans, maybe then he could avoid fighting the big battles where their horse soldiers would be involved. If he could work it out so that he was able to pick the area where the fighting would be held, he would demand an open field where the ground was rough and full of potholes to slow down the humans' horses.

He was now feeling much better. Having a working plan always brought him back to his good nature.

The only problem that he could see with using his personal

human slave girls as diplomats was that it would be better if he did not bed them. Sex and diplomacy did not seem to mix very well.

He would set up an appointment with Numbers One and Two for a meeting only, and then send them on their way. After that he could take his time and look at some of the new human slave girls about which he had heard one of his guards talking.

He was humming a little tune by the time he finished his walk and returned back to his command area.

# CHAPTER THIRTY-SEVEN

Atia was pacing back and forth in front of the council. It was several weeks now since the attack on his son Avoti had occurred, and things had been very peaceful since then.

Mog had sent a message to the human council that he had a proposition he wanted to present to them that might end the problems between humans and Neanderthals.

Over Atia's objections, the council had agreed to listen to what the Neanderthals' representatives had to say, and that had been several hours ago, in the early hours of the day.

There was quite a shock when one of the two human female diplomats came to the council meeting walking arm in arm with Atia's bodyguard, whom everyone simply called X.

X had formally arrested the other female diplomat and had her removed from the meeting room. He had shocked them all by telling them that the young lady whose hand he was still holding was his daughter who had been taken away by the Neanderthals when his settlement had been overrun some years ago. X told everyone that he thought she was dead and he never thought he would see her again. He said he was simply thrilled to have her alive and back with him.

The story of how she had worked herself up to being in Leader

Mog's good graces held them all spellbound. Finally, after several hours had flown by, it was obvious that the girl was exhausted, so they called an end to the meeting. They would meet again in the morning after Char, which was Number Two's human name, had rested.

Char and X walked out of the meeting room, just talking away. They were hanging onto each other, and it was a wonderful thing to see. For once a sad story had a happy ending.

Avoti was sure that tomorrow's meeting would be an eye-opener for all of them. Here was an insider Neanderthal diplomat who knew all the various secrets of the enemy, and she was now on their side of the conflict.

She seemed to be bursting with information that they were dying to hear. The discussion would cover all kinds of inside stuff on the workings of the Neanderthal society and how their army was set up. It should be an exciting meeting.

Something like this would be a thunderbolt. Insider information was going to be given to them from a most reliable source, and they could not wait for the time to pass.

Meanwhile Atia, who had a few hours to kill before he met with Ava for their dinner, walked over to the training area and sat to watch the foot soldiers working on their difficult coordination within the walking squares.

Atia was well aware of the great difficulty of coordinating a four-sided square with one hundred men per side shooting arrows outside that square at a pretend enemy, while being inside a larger square of one hundred and fifty men per side. There was a total of six hundred men who were there to protect the inside shooters with their long spears. The coordination for all of this seemed almost impossible to Atia.

Atia wanted to talk with Avoti about his high hopes for the semi-secret weapon whenever his wandering son decided to come home.

199

Atia was hoping that his son would follow him in the council one day, and he liked keeping him up on all the many changes that were happening all around them on a daily basis.

A quiet and thoughtful Atia turned around to retrace his steps on his way to meet Ava and have dinner.

# CHAPTER THIRTY-EIGHT

An absolute silence came over the huge crowd of people who had squeezed into the large council meeting room to hear what Char, daughter of X, had to tell them.

It was standing-room only, and the building was surrounded by hundreds of other humans who were standing outside waiting to hear what was going on inside.

The council had put out the word that Char, one of the two arriving diplomats from the enemy, was, amazingly, unknown to the Neanderthals as the daughter of X. This could be the special insider information that the humans all had been hoping to hear.

Everyone knew that the war was coming, and coming soon. This meeting might be the one that brought out the final information needed to attack the Neanderthals where they could hurt them the most.

It was further told to everyone that Char, who was called "slave girl Number Two," was taken away from her home settlement when it was overrun and destroyed by a raiding Neanderthal party several years ago. It had happened on a day when X, one of the leaders of that settlement, was away with a hunting party. He never thought that he would see his daughter again. Yet here she was as a full diplomat from the enemy.

Everyone was anxious to hear the vital information that she was going to tell them about the weaknesses of the enemy.

It was whispered about that she was the sex slave to the Supreme Leader Mog, and that it was this same Mog who had personally attacked Atia and nearly killed him.

Another unbelievable part of the story was that it was X who had saved Atia from Mog's deadly attack, and that made the testimony from X's daughter even more exciting.

Sitting at the front table with everyone's attention on them were Char, her father X, Leader Atia, the three generals of the different army sections, and a scribe who would be writing down each and every word that was spoken at this most important of meetings.

X introduced Char to everyone sitting at the front table and, after a few minutes of small talk, they all took their seats and looked over at Atia. He stood up and smiled warmly at his wife Ava and his son Avoti; both were seated in the front row center section of the crowded room.

Atia put up his hands and called for silence, and the room became absolutely silent as Atia slowly walked around the front table and stood facing the audience. He began to speak in his usual strong and clear voice that commanded everyone's attention.

"For those of you who do not know me, my name is Atia. I have been honored to have been elected as speaker for the important leaders who are all assembled here. We are here because a once-in-a-lifetime event has happened that, in our wildest dreams, we could never have imagined. It is my understanding that just about a little over three years ago, our enemies, the Neanderthals, attacked and totally destroyed one of our outpost settlements south of here. All human males were put to death, the settlement was burned down, and all the women and female children were taken away as captives and slaves. There is a very special person who is deeply involved in my life. This person has suddenly become the focus of a lot of attention. Many months ago, we received information that the

Neanderthals were going to go back on the offensive with a program of trying to kill off our leaders, myself included among them. I believe it was coming from the same old saying that if you cut off the head, the body will die. Well I was the head, and it was Mog, their Supreme Leader, who came after me personally to kill me. It was only by the heroic actions of X , whom our tribe insisted I use to be my personal bodyguard, that my life was spared. Because of him, I am now able to help organize our offensive war against the brutes that have made our lives into a living nightmare. It just so happens that Char, our own X's daughter, was one of the young girls carried off by the Neanderthals after they destroyed her home settlement. Obviously, Char is just as strong-willed and determined as our own X, and she somehow worked her way up the slave ladder to gain the confidence of Leader Mog. Char had been living among our enemy Neanderthals for many years, and she has learned the ins and outs of their daily lives, military abilities, and their hopes and fears. However, she did it or whatever she had to do to get it, she landed the important post of diplomat. She got herself and one other female human sent here to try to work out a treaty with us on behalf of the Neanderthals. Char has already told us one very important fact, even before we got into any discussion upon any other matter. She told us that the offer of a peace agreement by Leader Mog is a big lie and is meant to allow him time to build up his army with our destruction in mind. We will all hear from Char's own lips about her personal experiences among the Neanderthals and, hopefully, about her insight into the extermination of our enemy. I could go on and on about the many things we will shortly be doing, but we are all here to listen to Char. And now it is my pleasure to introduce you to Char, daughter of our very own comrade in arms, X."

With a smile on her pretty face and a wave of her hand, Char sat down on the edge of the stool that she had carried up with her. She seemed relaxed as she looked about the room and broke the silence with a fine-sounding voice.

"Hello, everyone; as you all must know by now, I am the daughter of the man you all call X.

I have been asked to keep my talk brief and to the point. I want to tell you about our common enemies and what we can all expect from them.

"So that I don't miss any important points, my dad and I wrote everything out. We have a copy for each of you to pick up after the meeting. We want you to spread these copies to anyone and everyone who is not here today. It will help unite us in our war against the Neanderthals. I am just going to read from the report and offer no comments at this time."

T IIΓ ҥ T

"This report has been written by Char, daughter of X, who is the chief of personal security for Leader Atia.

"At the age of thirteen and a half, my home settlement was attacked and burned to the ground by a roaming band of Neanderthals.

My father was away on a hunting trip at that time and that saved his life. My mother died that day from an arrow shot by one of the invaders.

"I was rounded up with twenty-seven other young girls and women and marched away from the settlement.

We were stripped of all of our clothing and had to walk naked throughout the forests. They did allow us to wear our shoes to protect our feet.

On the way to the Neanderthal camp, I counted nine times that I was raped, and each attack was more brutal than the one before it.

My hatred for the Neanderthals has grown each day, and I promised on my dead mother's memory that I would one day get revenge.

Hopefully this is the time for my revenge.

"The rest of the females and I arrived at the Neanderthal camp. After being allowed a few days to rest up and get our strength back, we were given to different families to work as household slaves.

I understood by talking to some of the other slave girls that my being whipped only once a day was easy when compared to them. There was nothing I could do to better my living conditions, and it was a living hell for well over two years in the same household.

I made it a point to learn as much as I could about the army of the Neanderthals so that if escape were ever possible, I would know some valuable things.

"One day a week, I was given a day off to myself. I would walk over to what I would call a tavern, which they called a refreshment center.

Since I did not care if I were raped by my household owner or by one of the local soldiers, I offered my body to a different soldier every time on my days off. Even though they tried to be gentle with me, they were still Neanderthal males, and I was always pretty badly abused, but I learned a lot about·their army.

"I learned that they had problems fighting as a unit with other Neanderthal soldiers. They had problems getting their extremely thick fingers around the string of a bow. Supreme Leader Atia's leading weapon makers were very excited about my confirming what they had hoped. They would continue making the longbow, which would give our bowman the extra ten yards in distance, keeping it out of the lesser range of the enemy.

"Another one of my bed partners told me that his band of wandering Neanderthals was attacked by human horse soldiers. The Neanderthals are terrified by the horses, and they always leave the battlefield if horses are involved in the fighting.

This soldier told me that Leader Mog is making plans to fight against horse soldiers only where the battlefield has large holes in the ground so that the horses will not be able to run there. Our commissioners have said that this is important to know so that our horses will only be led to fight on mostly flat areas. This is going into our commissioners' battle plans, and I am pleased that this information is important to them.

"Another important thing that I learned early in my captivity was that Leader Mog had taken one of the human slave girls, whose name was Kat, and made her his personal slave.

It was said that she was treated exceptionally well and was allowed to walk around everywhere quite freely. It took me a while, but I finally found out where I could see her wandering about the army camp so that I could see what she looked like.

"I saw that I was about the same height as Kat, but she walked and held herself in a different way. The way she walked just oozed sex, and I watched her all that day and all of the other days that I had off.

On some of my days off, I practiced wearing clothes like she did, which let my breasts hang out, and I was finally able to adjust my walk to look like hers after weeks and weeks of practice.

To get used to my new look, I would dress up or down like Kat did on my days off, when I would spend time with the tavern crowd. I was a great hit with all the soldiers who came in there.

Soldiers would fight over who would sleep with me. Since I was always available, and I was going to be attacked by some beast-man anyway, I spent my time having sex with these front-line soldiers listening to everything they could tell me about army life. After a long time of doing this, I got so used to being raped that it just seemed to be a way of life to me.

"I wish to say a word or two about rape here.

This is usually thought of as an unwanted sexual attack upon a female by an overly-aggressive male, but was I truly being raped when, of my accord, I went after the soldiers so that I could pick and choose the ones that I would bed down with? After a while, I actually used to look forward to my days off so that I could get laid by someone of my own choosing.

"To continue with my story, I found out the usual places where Leader Mog went when he had free time. I made myself available to be seen by him as he moved about, and I finally caught his wandering eye as he became aware of me. After all, I now looked like his recently deceased female human slave, Kat. I walked like Kat, and I was prepared to give him great sex like Kat did. I soon became one of his two 'new girls.'"

"The other new girl whom Mog had selected also had a similar look to Kat, and we both became 'Mog's girls.'"

"From that time on our lives became much better. There were no more beatings, much better food, and we got sexy clothes to wear. It was a definite improvement for us both."

"I was called Number Two, and my partner became Number One. I did not want anyone to know my real name because you never know who might remember it from the old family settlement days. Anyway, Number One and I moved into Mog's large living quarters."

"It is true that Mog had a big sexual demand thing, but with the two of us sharing the sexual requirements it was really not too bad."

"The best part of all this was that I was able to hang around Mog's house when he met with his generals and formed his war plans."

"Once in a while Mog would give me to one or two of his generals to have sex with, but I really never cared. This way, I was always around, almost like a piece of furniture, and I got to hear every detailed plan, every new idea, every weapon and every curse word that was ever spoken by them."

"I will be giving everything I learned over to the Atia commission, and I know that what I have told you will be a great help in the war effort."

"What I will be getting out of all this is that my father and I will be given a fully armed escort to a settlement far away with enough riches for the two of us to live comfortable lives. Hopefully the two of us can start our new lives and live happily ever after. But my wishing to live happily ever after seems impossible, with the entire known world soon going to war."

"I am pleased to know that I have contributed to the war effort by my hard-earned insider knowledge of our enemy."

"My father, knowing that he saved the life of our beloved leader, will have a good memory of having done something that was outstanding."

"Thank you for reading this long report. It would be wonderful if you could pass it on to others."

"We must all stay united in our war against the horrible Neanderthals."

"Signed, Char, daughter of X."

# CHAPTER THIRTY-NINE

arly morning finds us within a locked-down and extremely secure second-floor workshop especially set up for Char, her father X, and three master craftsmen in woodworking.

There were security guards stationed all around the small building, including on the stairway leading straight up to the second-floor workroom. The humans, having learned the value of extra protection, were going beyond what was needed. After the Atia/Mog-attack incident, they all realized that they were overdoing it, but agreed that too much security was much better than not enough.

It was now six days after the huge collective gathering at the general staff meeting, and everyone in the room was very excited about what they were doing.

They had been working nonstop on making samples of the two new weapons that they all believed would make the difference between winning or losing the upcoming war against the Neanderthals. If the planned demonstration they had scheduled for after the noon hour went well, mass production would be kicked into high gear.

They all knew that the Neanderthals would not be sitting back and allowing the humans time to get themselves ready for the upcoming battle.

X, who had the complete confidence of Atia and the entire general staff, was hunched over a woodworking lathe, shaping a large wooden plank.

Char left her father's side and walked over to watch one of the three men working on a strange looking Y -shaped, thick piece of hardwood. The workman held it up for her to see and then handed it to her. She took the smooth and oddly shaped carved piece of wood from him, ran her hands over it, smiled, and handed it back to the sweating woodworker.

She smiled at him and walked over to the second of the three workbench areas, watching another skilled worker carefully cutting out a very unusual shape from the thick rubber-like material that he was working on. It looked like nothing more than a thick braided rope that was all knotted up.

Char left him and went over to watch the final part being readied for the demonstration. After satisfying herself that everything was coming along smoothly and that they would be ready for the upcoming demonstration, she gave X a kiss on the cheek and left the area to go back to her tent to rest for a few hours.

If things went well later that day, the father -daughter team would be on their way out of the war zone with lots of riches in their possession. They would have a warm and happy feeling that the two inventions they were going to demonstrate would help win the war and help to destroy the much-hated Mog and his Neanderthal monsters.

T̄ III̊ ̈II T̄

Portable chairs were set up in a shady area that was a short but safe distance away from the targeting area where all the demonstrations were to be held. Also being set up, about one hundred paces farther away from where the watchers would be sitting, were a dozen or more wide haystacks. Attached to the front of the haystacks were many Neanderthal-sized armored chest protectors taken from the bodies of Neanderthals who had been killed by humans over the years. They were set up in rows of six, the formation in which the Neanderthals usually marched.

Sitting in the observers' seats were Atia and his son, Avoti, three general staff leaders, the human council, and a few more interested supporters.

Atia's idea was to show off the new weapons to the leaders. They all said that if the two secret weapons were as good as Atia said they were, they would get things going in mass production. Everything depended upon how the demonstrations went.

It was X who walked over to the observation area and asked for everyone's attention.

"Good afternoon, everyone. I would like to tell you what you will be seeing shortly. I can, possibly, answer any questions that you might have. Please hold your questions until the end of the demonstration."

"The demonstration will be in two parts. The first part will be on something that the inventors call a 'Sling Shot' and the second on what is called a 'Ballistic Device'."

"I know that right at this moment those are just words that mean nothing at all to you, but I promise you that in a few minutes you will never, ever forget them."

"In a few minutes Char will be passing out to each of you a special report to help you remember what you will be seeing here today. Right after everyone has the report, we will begin the demonstration."

"Thank you."

A smiling Char took a few moments to pass out the documents. She was pleased to see that almost everyone began to look at the report as soon as they got it. This showed her that there was great interest in the project. Char was thinking that if everything went according to plan, the object that they were about to demonstrate, and the following demonstration, could change the makeup of the world for all time.

The report read as follows:

1. *The Neanderthals have the biggest advantage in their size and in their strength. In any one-on-one fight with a human, the Neanderthal will most often win; therefore, it is most important to have our soldiers avoid any and all individual fights with the enemy.*

*Absolutely at no time will a human soldier be allowed to leave the company of other humans to whom he is assigned.*

*This means that if our humans stay together as a fighting unit, they will have the advantage over the enemy who will be fighting alone. The humans will always have the larger numbers in any encounter.*

2. *We have learned that the enemy is very much afraid of our horse soldiers and that they will leave the field of battle if they see horses coming at them.*

*We have received reliable information that they plan to meet us on a battlefield with many large potholes, which will cause our horses to become unusable; therefore, we will be using the horse soldiers only as a finishing-up force.*

3. *Our archers, with the recently developed longbows, can outshoot the Neanderthals by at least ten yards, therefore, our archers can stay back at least ten additional yards farther than they normally would. By doing this the enemy arrows will fall short by a ten -yard margin while ours will still be on target.*

*Our strategy will be to first use our archers, who will shoot and be shot back at by the enemy archers. By staying back the extra ten yards, which we have mentioned, our human archers should have few if any losses due to enemy arrows.*

4. *Next, we plan to turn loose our two new weapons on the enemy and reduce their number of fighters significantly.*

5. *The follow-up to the two new weapons will be to call in our well-*

*trained fighting squares, which should be able to finish off most of the remaining enemy soldiers.*

*After the Neanderthals meet with the fighting squares, we believe the enemy will go into complete retreat. As soon as they flee from the potholed battlefield, our horse soldiers will come pouring out of the surrounding hills to hopefully destroy all that is left of the enemy.*

The following information, which is for your eyes only, is about two newly developed secret weapons:

1. THE SLINGSHOT. This is a very small hand -powered projectile weapon. It consists of a Y-shaped frame held in the hand with two rubber-like strips attached to the upright sticks. The far ends of the rubber strips lead back to a pocket which holds a projectile to be shot at the enemy.

The holding pocket is grasped by the dominant hand and drawn back to the desired extent to provide power to the projectile.

Please see the following rough picture of a slingshot, which is a most dangerous weapon.

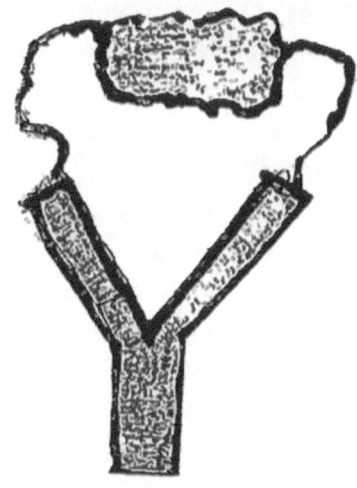

We believe that the slingshot will become the weapon of choice for our front-line soldiers.

It is extremely lightweight, can be easily attached to a holding belt, and can, basically, shoot a deadly projectile twenty to thirty yards with great accuracy.

It is believed that a stone shot from a slingshot will easily kill a Neanderthal with a properly fired shot to the head.

The average time it takes for one of our soldiers to properly learn how to use the slingshot is thirty minutes.

2.) THE BALLISTA or CATAPULT. This works exactly like the slingshot, only it is much larger and can be loaded with dozens of projectiles.

The way the second secret weapon came into being was that if a small rock or stone traveling at a great speed could kill one enemy, then why not build a bigger slingshot that would be able to kill several of the enemies with one shot?

It is believed that one shot from a well-aimed ballista can take out up to a dozen Neanderthals at a time.

The plan is to surround the battlefield with ballistas and, after firing off several rounds of killing material at the enemy, to follow up with individual slingshot shooters and bowmen to destroy any of the Neanderthals still standing.

In closing this report on our two new killing weapons, it must always be remembered that the best killing weapons of all time are our human fighters. They seem to have kept all of the deadly fighting abilities, rage and skills of our ancestors, who had to establish their right to survive in this harsh and deadly world of ours.

Our soldiers know that they are fighting for the rights of their women and children and for themselves to be able to live in this wonderful world of ours once we get rid of the hated enemy.

Thank you for your attention. Char, daughter of X.

# CHAPTER FORTY

A hush fell over the onlookers once again as Atia stepped forward, holding one of the newly crafted slingshots in one of his hands. In his other hand he was holding a small stone about three inches around.

Twenty yards away, Avoti had set up a bullseye target, which was leaning on three legs that were holding it in an upright position. Avoti dashed back to his seat in the front row as Atia began to speak.

"I practiced with the slingshot for several hours yesterday and about an hour this morning. I wanted to personally show you all how easy it is to shoot one of these things. I hope that I don't make a fool of myself by missing the target, but let me show you what this innocent-looking stick, some rubber and a piece of rope can do."

Atia slowly took the slingshot and held it at the base of the Y-shaped stick. He then took the three-inch stone and put it into the holding pouch. He slowly pulled back on the pouch with the stone in it, took careful aim and let go with the stone which flew on its way toward the standing target.

Atia's intent was to hit the bullseye, but that did not happen. The stone flew straight and true and hit the target about two feet to the right of the bullseye. None of the watchers knew or cared where it hit, because upon making contact, the entire target was blown back about ten feet and was shredded to pieces.

Even though Atia did not hit the bullseye, he completely destroyed the entire target.

Avoti, followed by the others, scrambled to his feet screaming and jumping for joy.

The weapon really worked, and they knew that if a piece of rock or some other hard object were to strike a Neanderthal like that, the fight would be all over for that enemy.

Hugs, screams and tears finally slowed down, and everyone

was reseated. X, with Avoti helping him, rolled out a ten-foot high duplicate of the small handheld slingshot that was just demonstrated.

X and Avoti made a great show of loading dozens of rocks and other sharp objects into the holding dish of the ballista.

While the two men were filling up the ballista, other helpers had set up a dozen haystacks with Neanderthal body armor facing toward the ballista and the audience.

The helpers scrambled out of the way. X was standing next to the pull lever of the ballista. He said softly as if he were talking to himself, but his voice carried well across the assembled audience, "I am pretending in my mind that those haystacks and empty uniforms are Neanderthal soldiers. I am pretending that they are the same Neanderthal soldiers who raped and killed my wife, my friends, and other humans who are dear to us all."

"I only wish that this were the real enemy out there and not just a few stacks of hay."

"I am pulling this release for myself and for all of you. This is what we are going to do to those Neanderthal bastards." X pulled the release, and a mild booming sound was heard as the projectiles flew perfectly straight to their intended targets.

The hay piles now were scattered, and the Neanderthals' armor were punctured full of holes.

The force of the contact knocked the targets back a number of feet. All that was heard from the onlookers was a gasp and unbelievable silence before a loud cheer went up that must have echoed for miles.

It was obvious to everyone that the demonstrations were a huge success. Everyone came away with tremendous hope in their hearts for a better world and a better future.

A human victory seemed possible at last, and Atia, the generals and the council were never as popular as they were at this time.

It was true that the entire settlement and all the neighboring ones around it would shortly be turning out a great amount of the new weapons. Everything seemed to be moving along nicely for the war effort. All of this was very pleasing to Atia.

Atia, however, had one last problem that was really bothering him. His latest problem was a family one. He had spent a great deal of time talking about it with the love of his life, Ava. It was Ava who had brought the issue front and center.

With her woman's thoughtfulness and deep understanding of what was going on in the world around them, she presented her thoughts to Atia who immediately agreed with her. Atia wondered why it was Ava, and not himself, who was able to recognize this issue that needed to be addressed.

It was Ava who brought up the subject of their getting on in years, saying that they were both slowing down.

Ava reminded him that when he was just about Avoti's age he had aggressively come to her clan. He seemed so strong and wise that he had just caused her to fall in love with him.

She asked if he remembered the night the clan was attacked by the Neanderthals who came to burn the crops that were growing in their special valley. She asked if he remembered his rage against the invaders which caused him to slaughter them and chase them back to the mountain of the cave bear.

She said he was young, strong and reckless in those years. She had loved him then, and she loved him now. Ava's concern was that she did not see the manly aggressiveness of Atia's early years in their son, Avoti, who, in her opinion, was not strong enough to take over the leadership from Atia within the next few years.

She said Avoti was a wonderful child: sweet, loving and everything a child should be. But in this violent world that they now lived in, it was not enough if he and the tribes were to survive the many problems that would be coming at them.

She said that there was no one better suited to bring out the Atia kind of strength and warrior boldness in Avoti than Atia himself.

She said that he had to make a cunning, clever and strong

leader out of their only son, and she said that he had to do it now.

Ava said that Atia needed to get tougher with Avoti and make him into the man who could follow in his father's footsteps. She suggested that Atia go into some form of warrior and leadership training with their son, and again Atia agreed with her, although he was not sure how to go about it. This was Atia's newest problem, one that he knew he had to solve soon for the good of everybody. A lot was riding on the young and capable shoulders of Avoti, son of Atia.

# CHAPTER FORTY-ONE

Over the following few weeks, Atia was an extremely busy man.

He was involved every morning with getting enough slingshots and ballistas into the hands of the army generals so that they could begin training the troops in the skills needed to effectively use the weapons.

The general staff was quite satisfied with the walking squares, the horse soldiers, the archers and the exciting new weapons which they were all counting on to bring them the expected victory.

The best and most educated guess was that in four months, which would be in the month of June, the weather would be warm and dry enough for them to attack the enemy. They only hoped that the Neanderthals would also wait for better weather before they took the field against the humans.

The human battle plans were still in the planning stages, but they would be ready to go within the timeframe that they all had agreed upon.

Atia was able to step away from the weapon and battle planning because that was the responsibility of the army.

His problem was that he only had a few months to complete the training of his son in the art of war.

Atia and Avoti began spending all of their time together. It was a rare thing for one of them to be seen without the other. The two of them spent hours and hours working with sword, spear and knife until Atia had to admit that Avoti, being younger and faster, had now passed him by.

Sad as he was that his own skills were losing their sharpness, Atia was happy with the progress Avoti was making.

Atia realized that he could only take him so far in the training of martial arts, which he still needed if he were going to take over as leader.

Atia put out the word that he was looking for the roughest, toughest, and most underhanded rough-and-tumble fighters in all of the settlements. He promised them a big payment if they had the teaching skills he was looking for. He ended up with experts in all types of the killing ways, and he hired them all.

One exceptional swordsman taught Avoti how to really use a sword and an axe. The use of these two weapons was more than mere strength and fancy moves. He was taught to be skillful, as well as cunning, thoughtful, and very, very dangerous. He was taught how to fight like a gentleman and to understand all the rules of proper conduct.

But what he needed most of all to learn, and it came easy to him, was how to fight dirty and how to use anything that came to hand as a weapon. He learned to scratch, gouge, maim and murder with his bare hands if he had to.

He was becoming the rough, tough young leader the tribe would need in future years.

One slim fellow taught him how to kill an opponent with just his hands in an unarmed combat. He even learned to kill with his feet, which was considered amazing. He learned to fight without a weapon against an armed opponent and how to win.

One of his teachers taught him to improve his knife skills by teaching him to accurately throw deadly blades.

220

A giant of a teacher showed him the tricks behind defensive weapons and how to attack and defend against an enemy on horseback.

And finally, at the end of it all, Avoti became colder, harder and tougher. In other words he was just about ready to be a leader among men.

𝕋 𝕀𝕀𝕀 𝕀𝕀𝕋

Weeks later Avoti left the settlement. Everyone had agreed that there was nothing more than any of them could teach him about murder and mayhem. They all said that he was a walking and talking fighting machine.

It was Atia who told Avoti to leave the settlement and go out to one of the areas where bands of Neanderthal raiders were last seen. He was to bring back a trophy from each dead Neanderthal to show the community that he was ready.

And so it was that Avoti and a band of four Neanderthals got into a fight to the death.

They met not too far away from where the earth ramp that Avoti remembered so well.

The four Neanderthal warriors laughed and made fun of the one human who dared stand up against the four of them, but the sounds of their laughter quickly changed.

Again, and again his weapon swung and, with each sweep, another hideous victim writhed in his personal agony while his brains or body parts oozed life's blood.

Avoti was feeling invincible, with a new strength surging through his limbs. He felt that his spirit was infused by some powerful force that seemed as if it had always been a part of him.

The Neanderthals screamed out their agony and tried to escape from the merciless axe that was constantly moving all around them.

Avoti's use of the double-sided and deeply-sharpened battleaxe was second only to his love of his sword.

Avoti's lips were drawn back in an atavistic snarl as he felt the blood of his primitive ancestors flood through his body. He seemed to sense that he was no longer alone within himself. This was something he would have to explore at a future time. Right now, he was too busy to think about anything other than killing Neanderthals.

Countless generations of hate urged him on and became a part of him. He was almost a spectator to the massacre that he was causing.

It was as if his arms were not his own, as if the heavy battleaxe was directed by a force which was beyond his control.

This was Avoti's moment in time, and the slaying of the enemy was his mission. He struck out mechanically, his body unhampered by any thoughts at all except to kill and kill again.

The bodies of his enemies lay sprawled across the floor of the killing ground.

Then, almost abruptly, there were no more standing enemies. All the Neanderthals were either dead or dying.

The expression on his face, which had been of murderous violence, relaxed, and his mouth curled into a contented and happy boyish grin. He wiped at the sticky blood that coated his face and body. It was not his blood, and the dead had no more need for it. He washed it off in a nearby stream.

With a happy smile on his face, he returned to the slaughter area and cut off the left ear of each of the fallen Neanderthals. His father had asked him to bring him some evidence of how his lessons had gone, and he carefully placed the ears into one of the bags that he had hooked onto his belt.

He was thinking about one of his father's favorite sayings that seemed to apply right now.

"Fortune favors the brave."

# CHAPTER FORTY-TWO

Supreme Leader Mog was not a happy Neanderthal. He had sent two of his best slave girls to work out a deal with the humans hoping for a conference to talk about the differences between them. Not a word had been heard from either of them within the allotted thirty days, so he had to assume that there would be no sit-down discussions, which he was hoping would buy him some time.

He then called for a meeting with his military leaders to see if any new ideas had occurred to any of them, but, as usual, all they could suggest was to attack and kill as many humans as they possibly could in an all-out mass attack.

He agreed with their basic idea but disagreed with just charging across the field of battle to meet the enemy. Things did not work that way anymore.

He tried to explain to them that the art of war had been changed forever, but it was like he was talking to the wall for all the good it did.

He knew that he had no one else around him who could help him with any of the needed planning. He could only count on himself. He finally received a special letter which had been fired into his command area by an arrow. This had been prearranged, so he knew something important had come up with the enemy. He had the special reports delivered in this fashion so that no one, neither Neanderthal nor human, could ever tell who the sender was.

One of the first things that Mog had done when he had won the title of Supreme Leader was to hold several secret meetings with a specific human whom he had known for many, many years. This human acquaintance had worked himself up to the level of councilman, and for many riches given to him privately by Mog, he had become his inside man for all these years. His inside human contact would not send him a note unless something of the greatest importance had come up.

He needed to sit down immediately and read the report from his spy in the camp of the humans. Mog entered his most private space and closed off all the openings. He gave instructions to his guards that he was not to be bothered for any reason.

He was hoping that something of great use would be revealed to him in this specially delivered mail. He opened the thick letter carefully so as not to tear any of the thin parchment on which it was written.

The note that Mog held with a shaking hand, read as follows:

*Hey Mog:*

*You sure screwed things up this time.*

*Remember those two young slave girls that you sent to the humans to see if you could put together a sit-down with them to talk about a peace treaty of some sort?*

*Well, my friend, one of the two females (the one you called Number Two) turned out to be the daughter of one of the main advisors to the leaders of the human council.*

*Needless to say she has been singing her little heart out about all the secrets you stupidly allowed her to listen to while you were so busy bedding her.*

*When I was alone with her for a few minutes, I asked her how you were as a lover and she said that you were the best Neanderthal male that she had ever slept with. I do think that this girl misses your loving, even though she did not come out and say so.*

*Anyway, the humans now know the size of your army, the weapons you will bring to the fight, and that the peace treaty you wanted to talk about was a big lie.*

*The other girl was locked up and is under guard so I could not talk to her.*

*Moving on for the moment, let me review a few things that you already know and a few other things that you should know but don't.*

*1. HORSE SOLDIERS—They outperform your soldiers by quite a lot, and, if you remember, I suggested earlier that you limit your contact with them to only a flat surface that has large holes in it so that the horses cannot run at you.*

*If you follow my suggestion and keep away from flat and smooth areas, your men should be fine.*

*2. BOWS AND ARROWS—Your best shooters will always come up at least ten yards short of the humans, who will stand back an extra ten yards and shoot away at your guys all day without getting themselves hurt.*

*Further suggestions:*

*Do not trade arrows with the human archers. They will wipe your soldiers out very quickly.*

*3. MARCHING SQUARES—they will hurt you, and hurt you badly. Keep away from them no matter what.*

*They will walk up to your people and shoot them up badly, and* because of the extra long spears on the outside squares, your men will not be able to get at them.

My suggestion here is that if your officers see one of the squares coming, have them get the hell out of there as fast as they can. Your soldiers can not stand up to these moving squares.

4.) THE HUMAN ARMY—They have come up with some sort of secret weapons that they say will end the war by themselves.

The demonstration for these two secret weapons is scheduled for tomorrow, and I will have a front-row seat.

Tomorrow night or the night after, one of my people will deliver the information you will need to know on these two new weapons, although I find it hard to believe that two new weapons can end this conflict between your people and mine, which has been going on for thousands of years.

By the way, and just so you will feel secure about no one else knowing about these special arrow notes, I will have my arrow shooter killed after he reports back to me that he has completed his assignment to you.

I am running out of reliable men to send on this dangerous task, so I want you to double your next payment to me. That way I can keep sending you the good information that you need

Please do not make any new military moves until I advise you as to what you will be up against after I see the two secret weapons.

I assume that after I tell you about your new problems, you will be able to figure out a countermeasure, as you always have in the past.

You will be hearing from me shortly.

Remember, make no moves until you learn what will be coming at you in the way of weapons.

Goodbye for now.

# CHAPTER FORTY-THREE

The main building for the headquarters of the leadership of the human army was located on the north-eastern side of the practice field. Security was heavy surrounding the area, and everyone and everything was on high alert.

Late yesterday afternoon two Neanderthals waving a white flag of truce had approached the outpost of the settlement and had left a package with the guard to deliver to Atia and the council of the humans. They said that there was an important note from Supreme Leader Mog to be delivered to the human leaders. The two Neanderthals then turned around and headed back into the thick wooded area from where they had come.

The letter had gone through several hands before it was delivered to Atia by his personal aide. Without opening it, Atia had called for an immediate emergency meeting to take place the next morning at first light in the headquarters.

He had invited the council, the army generals, Avoti, Char, X, and extremely heavy security.

He had based his assumption upon the nice spring weather that the whole area was now having and had come up with the thought that this was Mog's opening move in the drama of the war they all knew was drawing ever closer. It had been some seven weeks since the demonstration of the slingshot and the ballista.

This was enough time for all the weapons to have been made and for all the men to have had the proper training in the use and care of these new weapons.

Atia had gone over and over in his mind what the humans had going for them in the upcoming battle against Supreme Leader Mog's soldiers.

He reviewed them all, one by one, in his mind's eye.

1. The Horse Soldiers—very effective and a very strong weapon to use but needed a flat and smooth area for the horses to be a factor.

2. The Archers—very effective and should be able to outshoot the enemy if they kept themselves at the proper distance.

3. The Marching Squares—they were thought of as being completely unstoppable and would be the last out on the battlefield.

4. The Slingshots and the Ballistas—these were believed to be the ultimate weapons and they were being counted on to completely destroy the bulk of the huge Neanderthal battle formations.

5. Following Directions—also going for them was the fact that humans had no problems taking orders from other humans called officers.

Char had assured them all that the Neanderthals would be fighting against the human forces as individuals or as small groups.

With all of the above facts running through his head, he tried to visualize, once again; all the possible large enough battlefields that were available within the immediate area of the Neanderthal forces and his own.

There were only six or seven possibilities and he knew that he could throw out five of them immediately. They were perfect for humans with mostly long, flat areas and only slight rises in the surrounding hills. Since they would be perfect for human needs, he knew that Mog would find them unacceptable.

Char had told them that any battle that was going to take place would only be in an area potted with large holes and breaks in the ground.

That left only two possibilities, and knowing this, he and the generals had ridden out to the two land areas to explore them. Each had taken the assignment that if they were in charge of the Neanderthal forces, where would they want to fight the battles so that the humans and their horses would be neutralized?

They had all agreed upon the one spot that backed up to the Neanderthal side of the area, had very few surrounding hills, and many, many large potholes all over the place.

It would be the perfect fighting place for the Neanderthals. All of the generals and Atia were very confident that this would be the area that Mog would pick.

They all went back to the human settlement knowing pretty much where the Neanderthals and humans would meet each other in the opening battle, and they made their plans accordingly.

The human leaders were meeting in the early morning of the day after Mog's note was handed over to Atia. Atia was now opening the note that had been delivered to him. There was absolute silence in the room as he cleared his throat and began to read.

"Greetings, human leaders. First of all I wish to extend my apology to Leader Atia for my having tried to kill him.

I was having a bad day, and I really did not think it through. I also apologize for another attack that was made on Atia's life by one of our female human slaves.

Please understand that I did not authorize the human female named Kat to attack. She thought that she would please me by going after him, but it ended up in her life being taken from her.

"Moving forward with the reason for this note, the world of the Neanderthals and the world of the humans do not seem to be able to get along with each other. Therefore, I am suggesting that we have a small, quick and exciting fight. I am suggesting that we use the battlefield that backs up to the beginning of the forest leading to where the Neanderthals live. I am sure that you know this place because it is the one where you were seen walking.

"Here is my offer. I know that there is little trust between us, but maybe there is something that we can agree to. The winner of this small battle, which will be limited to two thousand troops on each side, will become the dominant ruler of this entire section of the continent.

"If the humans lose, it is expected that you will leave this area and move everything and everyone far, far away into the southern part of our continent.

"If the Neanderthals lose, then we will pick up everything and everyone and move south.

"This will not end the conflict between our two peoples, but it will give us all some time to work out another plan so that we might all learn how to live together in the future.

I know it sounds like a plan that may be hard to accept, but it seems to be better than the open war we have had against each other for years and years beyond count.

"Whether you agree to this plan or not, please let me know within thirty days.

Please send back your message to me with my human female diplomat that you have locked up. I call her Number One. She is innocent of ever having done anything against you humans. She is one of my favorite humans and I would like her back.

"SUPREME LEADER, MOG"

# CHAPTER FORTY-FOUR

Atia put the message down and looked around at the dozen or so people sitting and watching him. He thought carefully about what he was about to say. "Gentlemen, one of us attending this meeting is a traitor. He or she is not just a traitor for our war against our enemies the Neanderthals, but a traitor against all humankind.

Before I accuse anyone I wish to state the evidence that has led me to this conclusion.

"Char has told us that all Neanderthal archers are now, suddenly, being equipped with a body shield to use when our enemy arrows are incoming against them.

Someone has told them about our use of the longbow, which gives us the extra yards we need to be successful.

Mog has given each of his archers this new shield because he knows beyond a doubt that, before his shooters can get close enough to exchange arrows with us, they will have to block our arrows. We all know that our arrows will go the extra yards beyond what the thick Neanderthal fingers can attempt.

"Horses with mounted soldiers were pretty much an unknown item to them before someone told them about our plan. Someone also told them about how our riders coordinate the horses' charge, and they are probably building defenses against us as I am speaking.

Only an insider would know this.

"Finally, and tragically, one of our new slingshot weapons is missing and only our three generals have unlimited access to our military supplies.

"This brings our list of suspects down to three."

Atia glared over at the three generals, who were all sitting perfectly still with only their eyes following Atia as he was speaking.

"I had a problem believing that a human being would sell out to the Neanderthals, but I realized that something very serious was going on, which I investigated myself.

"One of our generals has lost two of his staff members in the last few months. All other staffers are accounted for.

One of the missing staff members was seen recently walking out of the safety zone that surrounds our settlement. He was later seen silently returning to his sleeping quarters, and the very next day he was among the missing.

"Yesterday my daily count of all weapons came up short by one finished slingshot, so we now have one slingshot and one staffer that have not been located.

Either the human took the slingshot over to the enemy, or the slingshot was delivered to the Neanderthals, and then, upon that staffer's return, he was done away with so fingers could not be pointed at a general.

"I have a few more interesting points, but they will wait for a better time than this. I have said enough on this unpleasant subject, and I wish to move on to other things.

General Zarnath, if you would please remain seated after the meeting, it would be greatly appreciated."

The other two generals got up, gave General Zamath a weak smile, and moved away from him across the room.

Atia went on as if there were no interruption.

"We must assume that the enemy has knowledge of our secret

weapons. It goes without my having to say it, but obviously, our secret weapons are no longer secret.

"I cannot think of what the defense for the slingshot or the ballista could be, but as he has done in the past, Supreme Leader Mog comes up with things that always seem impossible. Therefore. now that this meeting is sort of secure, it seems reasonable for us to try to come up with a new plan for the battle since we will probably accept the offer that Leader Mog has made to us.

"We should release his female diplomat whom he calls Number One.

But now we shall play Mog's game and learn from his clever way of doing things.

"We will have to figure out a way to allow Number One to accidently see a sketch or hear a closed discussion on some sort of additional new secret weapon. Of course, we do not have any sort of new weapon, but neither Number One nor Mog will know that.

Mog will have to spend his time trying to stop our use of it against him, and that will take some time away from his planning to do other things.

"Gentlemen, we need to redo our battle plans before we accept Mog's invitation to fight.

But fight him we must, and we must fight to win."

# CHAPTER FORTY-FIVE

Mog was seated again in his secured work area. He had doubled the security all around him before he allowed himself to sit down and open up the bulky package that he had received in the usual secretive manner.

When he opened it, he was very surprised to see a funny shaped piece of wood with a rubber attachment on the top.

He had no idea what it was that he was looking at, and so he very carefully unwrapped the notes that came with the wooden thing.

He loved getting the general's notes. This package had been delivered to him two days ago, but this was the first chance he had had to sit quietly and read it.

The note read:

*Hey Mog.*

> *I got a good one for you this time.*
> *I know you will remember that I told you about the two secret weapons that the humans have.*
> *Well, here is one of them, and it is called a slingshot.*
> *I know that it does not look like much, but I want you to*

*try it out right now.*

*Put this down and go outside. Find a solid rock that is at least two inches around but no more than three.*

*Then come back and close the door so that no one can see you. Take the slingshot in your left hand and put the rock in the inside of the holding pouch on top of the wood. Pull the rubber pouch out and then let it go. Fire it at a tent wall or something that you don't need.*

*After that come back and read the rest of this letter.*

A very curious Mog followed the note's instructions to the letter. He put the note down, went outside and found what he thought was a two-inch round stone, came back into his room, and secured the door flap again.

He then picked up the wooden slingshot in his left hand, put the stone into the rubber pouch, balanced it so that it would not fall out, pulled back the rubber pouch that held the rock, and then let it go.

*WHAM! BAM!*

There was a hole in the tent wall about five or six inches wide and when he looked across at the tent next door, he saw another hole punched in its outer wall.

He had to sit down and review what had just happened. He had done it himself with a piece of wood, a stone and a bit of rubber.

*Unbelievable.*

He went back, picked up the rest of the report from the general, and continued to read.

*HEY MOG.*

*If you did it right, something got destroyed. If I am correct, then you are absolutely as amazed as I was when*

*I first saw it. At the time I was afraid.*

*Here is my question to you:*

*The humans have made these slingshots by the thousands, and they are now part of the equipment that every human soldier has on his body at every moment.*

*So how will you stop this flying stone from killing every one of your soldiers? I have no idea, and maybe you should try to sign a peace treaty with the humans. Now I have to tell you about the next secret weapon that they have come up with; it is called a ballista.*

*A ballista works just like the slingshot that you just held in your hand, only it is maybe a hundred times bigger I*

*Believe me when I tell you that they can perfectly control it, and they can shoot hundreds of rocks and other things from the ballista. Your men will not have a chance against it.*

*Again, I suggest that maybe a peace treaty is your best way to avoid sudden death.*

*There is no way to defeat these two weapons.*

*If you can find a way out, then you will be the smartest Neanderthal or human that ever lived.*

*Good luck. I will hear through my sources what you have decided to do.*

*This will be my last message to you until the war has either started or ended. It is just too dangerous for me to continue communicating with you.*

*Good luck.*

Mog ripped up the report to shreds so that nothing could ever be seen by anyone else about what was written here.

He needed to get some fresh air and do some thinking. He took the slingshot with him and promised himself that it would never be out of his sight again.

Whenever he needed to really think about something, he knew that getting laid did it for him. His head was always clearer after a wild sexual encounter. Only this time he wanted a wild female, wilder than any human female slave could ever be. He wanted and needed a female Neanderthal in all her grotesque beauty and wildness.

He headed for the part of the settlement where the single females lived.

He had a big smile on his face once again.

Thanks to his inside information, he knew exactly what the problem was and when he knew that, he always came up with an answer. This one presented him with a bit more to think about, but he was Mog, and Mog never gave up, never.

He continued smiling as he headed for the wild sexual encounter that he knew was ahead of him.

# CHAPTER FORTY-SIX

Later that afternoon, we find Mog wandering about the settlement's marketplace, enjoying a few hours of freedom, and being on his own with nothing in particular that he has to do except entertain himself.

In the back of his mind, he kept thinking about the letter from the general and the terrible problems that the slingshot and the ballista would cause on the battlefield.

Mog did his best thinking when he was distracted by doing something else, and he hoped that he shortly would have one of those ideal moments where everything fell into place for him.

His last thought upon the problem before he put it away was not how to avoid the weapons, or even how to make weapons of equal strength, but to somehow convince the humans that using them would be bad for them. He was not sure yet how he would do it, but making them not use the new weapons was the right answer. All he had to do was to figure that out.

He continued to walk about the local settlement's marketplace, sampling fresh fruit and other eating delights.

The many years of learning to place these kinds of major problems into the back of his mind had allowed him to now have some needed fun and relaxation.

He found it interesting that every time he offered to pay for something he wanted to eat, the vendors would bow and refuse to take his coins. Who he was seemed to be a well-known fact, and he was careful not to overdo things.

He moved along at a very casual pace and soon found himself wandering into the area where females were readily available for fun and games at a price.

It was the combination of different kinds of girls that fascinated him. He had never given something like this much thought, where, for a fee, he had his pick of females of all sizes and body types.

There were plenty of human female slaves whose masters put them here to bring in some money to pay them back for the food and lodging that was provided to them.

He saw "purebred" Neanderthal females in all their glory, showing a peek here and a peek there of what they had to offer. The Neanderthal girls normally interested him, but for now he didn't want their strong and bulky bodies. He could have these types of women anytime.

What he was really looking for was the best of the Neanderthal females and the best of the human females in a special combination that would give him the oversized breasts that he craved but on a much slimmer body to carry them. He thought that this would be a great package.

The hot sweltering air was quite humid and thick, but a slight breeze tugged at his hair and blew a little relief over the general area. When he looked up at the sun, he saw that it was its usual broiling white-hot ball in the sky, reflecting its heat off of everything.

Up to that moment nothing caught his wandering eye until he saw her standing there talking with a few of the other girls.

"Might I have your company for the rest of the afternoon, my dear young lady?" asked an interested Mog.

"Huh?" was the answer that he got back from Ruta, who had stopped her conversation and turned to look at him. There was instant recognition in her eyes of Supreme Leader Mog.

Ruta was one of those screaming female Neanderthals who had crowded into the packed areas where she saw him win the arrow-shooting contest, the spear-throwing contest, and the sword-fighting to-the-death contest with the human female Xan.

She remembered Mog quite well, as did all of her surrounding friends, and she was just simply overwhelmed when he spoke directly to her.

This seemed to be one of her life fantasies coming true where she and the Supreme Leader met, he swept her off her feet, and afterward she became his woman.

Ruta had heard all the wonderful stories about how Mog treated all of the women who lived with him. They were taken away from the day-to-day problems of having to scratch out a living on the busy streets of the settlement. They got to live inside the Leader's compound, wear fancy clothes, eat good food, and have the kind of life that would be the envy of all her friends.

After a moment or two of getting herself together, she found she was holding the arm of her newest and most famous client and leading him off to her rented place, where she did her finest work.

As she strutted off with Mog, she knew that all eyes were upon her. There would be lots to talk about later with all of the girls. Right now her heart was soaring as she made small talk with the Supreme Leader. They stopped outside of her small place.

Ruta was twenty-three years old and the daughter of a Neanderthal father and a human female slave.

Having no special skills but having a beautiful face and a full-figured body had led her to making a very comfortable living on the streets as a companion. She had learned to never say "no" to a client and, as a result, her business was good enough so that she could pick out whom she would give herself to. Her life was a good life, but she knew that there was more out there, and now here she was in that special moment she had always waited for.

She was hoping that she could keep Mog's interest after he took out his desires on her body. She would try to keep him interested enough so that he would keep coming back to her.

It was only minutes later that she closed the door behind them as she led him into her small bedroom.

He slid into the first kiss slowly, savoring the moment, knowing what it would do to both of them. He knew how the first taste of her would be for him, and he looked forward to it.

Ruta's lips bloomed open under his soft kiss, and she waited for the first eager thrust of his tongue. She felt the edge of one of his fangs at the edge of her mouth. It wasn't sharp, exactly, but it was quite pointed.

His mouth opened against hers, and he released a big sigh. She dipped her tongue into his mouth and brushed against his tongue fleetingly.

He tasted vaguely of expensive liquid. He smelled of rich leather clothing, and a little of warm wool, but he also had the smell of an aroused male Neanderthal which she quickly understood.

She felt her nipples tightening as she pressed her body deeper into him to get a better sense of who he was.

He walked them over to the large uncovered bed. They stood there at the foot of the bed while his tongue moved around with hers, teasing her with light in-and-out strokes.

His large hands cupped her hips and slowly drew her against him quite aggressively as he carefully nipped at her bottom lip with his long teeth.

Her hands slid around his neck, her fingers tangling in the silk of his black mane. Her knees spread wide to straddle his thighs, and her large breasts pressed firmly against the broad wall of his chest.

He stepped backward with a small smile covering his big face. "Kindly disrobe. I would like to see all of you."

Ruta grabbed the bottom of her top coverall and lifted it over her head. She tossed it to the floor away from the bed. She reached behind her and unfastened the bindings that were holding her beautifully formed twenty-three-year-old breasts in place. Mog stared fixedly at her breasts.

"Ruta, I find you very charming. If you are as good as I think you are, I would like you to join several other special girls that I have picked out. I would like you all to move into the settlement to live with me.

There is no need to answer right now. I still have to see you in action.

"Your body is beautiful, Ruta, and you remind me somewhat of an old favorite human friend of mine called Kat. Kat is no longer among the living. I'll tell you her story at another time.

Right now, I am waiting for the rest of your clothing to be discarded. I AM WAITING, RUTA."

She quickly began to unfasten the holders on her trousers, while she was thinking that life with Mog might not be as wonderful as she thought, *He wants what he wants when he wants it. He seems to be just like any other typical male. Living with Mog might not be the greatest idea in the entire world. He sounds awfully tough. Maybe that is why he is the Supreme Leader.*

Ruta stepped back and undid her pants. She was thinking that it had been forever since one of her customers had properly made love to her. Almost all of the males that she serviced were interested in their own needs and feelings.

Maybe Mog was different and she could get properly laid and enjoy herself for once. She knew that she would soon find out.

Before she realized it, Mog had thrown all of his clothing into a pile and stood there naked before her. He was quite the male specimen, and she knew that he knew it.

His arms closed around her small waist, pulling her tightly up against his body. She could feel the hard length of his erection pressing against her. She could not stop her nipples from peaking hard and just waiting to be suckled.

Mog pushed her head down, and she quickly understood what he wanted. He wanted a blow job.

She thought to herself, *Why am I not surprised?*

The Supreme Leader of all the Neanderthals was turning out to be just another Neanderthal male. She released the breath that she did not realize she was holding and dropped down to her knees.

*Let's see if I can do something differently and really surprise him,* she thought.

He pushed his big shaft down toward her waiting lips. Ruta stared at the big thing pointing at her and began to work her mouth to generate saliva. He was big, thick and long. She was not going to be able to deep-throat this monster. That meant keeping her hands on his hips to make sure that he didn't shove that thing any deeper than she could handle.

She licked her hands and reached out with both wet palms to smooth out the warm length of his shaft from head to root. He groaned out loud and began to take deep breaths.

*Oh,* she thought, *he seems to like that. Let's see how he likes this one.*

Ruta's smile broadened. She leaned forward with her wet tongue, straightened it and twirled it around the very top of his extended member. He tasted clean. She could smell the soap he'd used under the rich musk of male arousal that she was getting from him.

She widened the circling of her tongue until she stroked the flared edges, then took him deeper and deeper to the back of her throat.

She pulled back slowly while sucking strongly. He slid out of her mouth with the sound of wet suction. She did not push his hands away from her head as she wanted him to complete his sex act. She wanted Mog, Supreme Leader Mog, to know that she had taken him, a powerful male, over the edge of sexuality.

He was hers now; lost to this passion, lost to what she had taken away from him for the moment—control. And oh, how she loved it.

She could take any male, human or Neanderthal, and do her thing on him to sexually conquer him completely. It was as if she had the power of the world right there in her lips.

For that special moment, she was the supreme leader.

# CHAPTER FORTY-SEVEN

The blue sky burned once again overhead like a torch. Beneath it lay the vast, flat plains of the south-western portion of the land that separated the area of the Neanderthals from those of the humans. Here the land was absolutely flat, baked as hard as the floor of a baking oven.

Spread out here and there were potholes caused by some small animals that made their nests in and about the fields.

It was upon this large land area that the humans had agreed to meet the Neanderthals in one major battle to determine which of the two dominant groups would get to stay in the ancestral grounds and which would pick up and leave the entire area.

The humans knew that this pocketed field was chosen for the battle because it would effectively rule out the use of the human horse soldiers. They did not object to this because they were counting on the slingshot and the ballista to carry the day for them.

It was only a few days ago that Atia had called the two generals, the council, Char, X, and finally Avoti to meet with him at the central meeting place.

They were all deeply worried because they knew that the secret weapons were no longer secret, even though the last note from Mog to them did not make any mention of weapons of any type.

They all knew that the Neanderthals would show up in great numbers and fill their half of the battleground with tightly packed ground troops surrounded by their spearmen and archers. Unless there was something new that Mog was hiding from them, they were not too worried.

The human plan was very simple. On the human half of the field, they had lined up dozens of ballistas and each one had large supplies of perfect hurling stones.

When they tested the range area that the ballista could cover, they found to their absolute delight that the flying objects covered almost the entire center area where the battle would be fought.

Standing behind the ballistas were the archers, who practiced night and day, judging when they should release their arrows so that they would be able to strike at the enemy and yet still be ten yards beyond its returning firepower.

The plan was that after the ballistas had done their thing and the archers had shot their arrows, then the walking squares would cover the entire field and finish up any Neanderthals who were still walking around.

The horse soldiers would be the final part of the plan. They would be on the other side of the surrounding low hills, waiting for the order to charge. That order would finally come only after the Neanderthals were in full disorder from all the prior human attacks and were trying to flee from the flat battleground.

There was an extremely large patch of flat area of land that gave them good access between the wooded area of the Neanderthals and the beginning of the hole-pocketed area. It was during that part of the plan that any Neanderthals who were trying to escape back to the wooded area would be swept away by the horse soldiers.

At every discussion meeting and at each and every practice and walkthrough, the plan seemed to be one of simple perfection.

However—and it was a gigantic however—they also knew that Mog was well aware of the slingshots and the ballistas. Since he knew what to expect, why was he going to put his men out there when they would be facing certain death?

They all worried that there was something that Mog knew and they didn't. Mog must have something planned for them.

It was this great big potential problem that they did not even know about that caused all of them not to sleep well at night. They met with each other often to see if there was something they could come up with that was not already in their weapons' program.

The day finally arrived. It was the morning before the big battle, which was scheduled for noon the next day, that found them all together once again.

Atia was holding the final note from Mog, and they planned to go over it one last time.

This final reading was to be by Avoti so Atia could join the others and just listen to hopefully help them think of anything they had missed.

In a soft voice that carried well, Avoti began to read:

"To supreme leader, Atia:

"Greetings to you and to all the other humans on the council.
This will be my last written note to you before we meet on the battlefield.

"We Neanderthals will honor our agreement with you. Namely that the loser in this fight to end all fights will pack up everything and move far away to the warmer areas of the south.

"If we are on the losing side, we agree to the two-year timeframe to depart. It is rather sad knowing that although we are all men, we cannot get along with each other.

I truly believe that it is our basic nature, both

human and Neanderthal, that brings us all to this fight to prove which is the better, stronger, and smarter group.

"Our forces will be in place on or before the agreed-upon time, and I believe that you will also be ready. This starting time will give us all enough time to fight and allow the loser to withdraw from the field.

As we all agreed, nothing will be held back. Anything and everything goes.

"Please allow me to close with my repeated apology for that unwise and not proper personal attack that I made upon you.

Hopefully all that sort of thing is in our past.

"Supreme leader, Mog"

After another hour or so of the usual discussions, the group broke up and everyone went their separate ways in preparation for the big battle scheduled for the next day.

# CHAPTER FORTY-EIGHT

The human leaders were all gathered at the top of the high-est of the small hills behind the well-armed soldiers. Every-thing they could think of that needed doing was already done. Now it was time to just wait and see what the day held in store for all of them.

There were plans in place for following a defeated Neanderthal army back to their home base, and plans to hold back the winning Neanderthals if they came out of all of this as the winners. There was no doubt in any of the human leaders' minds that, unless Mog had come up with something that no one else had thought of, a victory was just waiting for the humans to claim.

The two armies were already on the field and moving about to get themselves ready. The humans were mostly sitting on the ground where they would be ready to fight at a moment's notice.

The Neanderthals had two unusual things going on in the area where they were gathered, which both surprised and worried the human leaders.

The first thing that they all noticed was a large raised platform standing about fifteen feet high. It was assumed that this was a viewing area for Mog and his officers from which to watch the battle. They would probably be sending orders out by messengers from this central control area to the formations.

The human command post was set up pretty much the same way except that they had gone one step further in their organization. They had divided their human warriors into six different sections with each section having a different color sash worn by the soldiers and their officers.

If, for example, the human commanders had an order for the red group, a messenger from the command post would rush over to the red group and give the order to the officer in charge of that particular location. Each of the human fighting groups had their own colors, which were black, blue, green, yellow and orange.

The Neanderthals were doing something different, also, which was that a large blocking sheet of material was in front of each Neanderthal as he marched out onto the battlefield and took up his position.

The materials that were covering the front of each Neanderthal group were gray in color and were about seven feet high. They were like huge banners being held up in front of each group of fighters. If they had wanted to block off the humans from seeing their men lining up, they were very successful. This lack of clearly viewing the enemy had the human leadership quite nervous. What could they possibly be hiding behind those gray banners? Was this somehow Mog's expected response to the slingshot and the ballista?

Everyone was extremely nervous as the time slowly passed on its way to high noon, which was the scheduled starting time for the war to begin. High noon was picked because there could be no mistake as to the time when the sun in the sky was at its peak for the day.

There was not much longer to wait as an ominous quiet descended across both sides of the battlefield.

One of the many things that bothered Atia was the fact that he was far behind the fighting lines and would not be able to see exactly what would be happening when the two armies clashed on the field.

He had also kept Avoti out of the fight, in that he was considered future leadership.

Leadership did not fight as common foot soldiers.

The soldiers were armed with knives, swords, bows and arrows, slingshots and some handheld spears which appeared here and there in the ranks.

Within minutes of the actual time of high noon, horns were sounded, and the human soldiers all got to their feet. The moment that they had all been waiting for had finally arrived. The soldiers all seemed rested and ready to fight as they tightened up their formations.

The battle plan was for them to advance only a little bit from their present positions. They were to go toward the middle of the field only far enough so that their lines were spread out evenly across the width of the area. They all knew to be very careful of the many potholes that were underfoot.

When the enemy was within firing range of the slingshot each soldier was now holding in a ready-to-fire position, the ballistas would fire and the field would be filled with flying material directed at the Neanderthals.

Besides the slingshots that each human held ready, a small shield was covering him in case of incoming arrow fire being directed at him. They had stolen this new idea from Mog. A great shout came bursting across the field as the Neanderthals received their marching orders.

The two sides very slowly picked their way across the pocketed ground.

The humans held their slingshots and shields in a ready position as they stood quietly and watched the slow advance of the Neanderthals. The Neanderthals slowly marched closer, with their blocking banners still held high and in place so that the humans could not clearly see the slowly advancing fighters.

Everyone was wondering why this strange thing was being

done, and they were only moments away from finding out the horrible truth that was waiting for them.

The covering banners were finally dropped and trampled underfoot by the slowly advancing enemy.

The front-line human soldiers, as an entire group, suddenly held back firing their ready-to-shoot weapons. Coming at them were two thousand Neanderthal soldiers, which were expected and very well prepared for. The human soldiers were waiting for them. The long-awaited fight that they had trained so hard and long for was now upon them, and they were ready, very ready.

They all stared in horror, however. They could not believe what they were seeing.

They now all knew what the clever thinking supreme leader Mog had come up with to counter the human advantage of the slingshot and the ballista.

What the human soldiers saw at the same moment, causing them all to back off from firing their weapons, was that each slowly advancing Neanderthal soldier had tied to the front of him a helpless, naked human female slave.

Each female was closely tied up, with her hands tied to the hands of each Neanderthal. They were physically attached and facing forward. Their feet were also tied ankle-to-ankle with the Neanderthals, so that each step and each

move made by the Neanderthal soldier was matched exactly by the closely bound female.

The women were the blocking shields for

the wickedly screaming Neanderthal soldiers as they marched forward in

perfectly-locked steps toward the lines of the humans. Their evil smiles were just beaming from their ugly faces.

They knew who had the advantage on the battlefield now, and they were enjoying themselves to the fullest.

Each female hostage had a thick gag tied tightly in her mouth to stop her from screaming and warning the waiting human troops.

Mog had come up with the plan of gathering each and every female human slave from all over the Neanderthal world so that he had plenty of female humans to satisfy his needs. He spent weeks training his soldiers to learn how to move about with females tied up in front of them.

He had ordered each female stripped of all clothing. Being naked was his way of showing the humans that all of the females attached to his men were human.

He thought that he knew humans well enough to count on them not firing their weapons against other humans, especially females. It turned out that he was right, and that decision on his part turned the tide of the battle that day.

Mog had gone even one step further. He had given permission for each soldier to rape the captive female human assigned to him as often as he wished. The females and the soldiers, however, had to be kept apart for a minimum of four days before the battle day so that they all could be back at full strength.

His troops loved Mog for giving them the use of the women, and his loyalty from his soldiers was one hundred percent.

Mog had given no consideration to raped and highly abused female humans because to him they were just battle protection for his all-important fighters.

As it turned out, the result of having the human females in front of his Neanderthals, facing the human troops, turned out exactly as Mog had predicted.

The humans did not fire their ballistas or their slingshots. Not one shot was fired anywhere.

Almost all of the human soldiers turned around and ran back toward the human settlements. They had no instructions as to what they were supposed to do in this situation, and so they just turned around and ran away.

The slowly advancing Neanderthals began firing hundreds of

arrows into the backs of the fleeing humans, killing and wounding scores of them.

It was all over within thirty minutes from start to finish, when a loud Neanderthal signal horn recalled the fighters back to camp. As ordered, they turned and started back toward their camp, singing victory songs as they moved along.

Mog had given standing orders for the soldiers to kill their still-attached human females, but most of the happy Neanderthal soldiers did not do so. It was true that the soldiers were beasts at heart, but as bad as they were, they were not bad enough to slaughter helpless females who had caused them no harm. These now-unattached females, most of whom were physically able to move and to help other former captives, followed the fleeing human fighters toward the safety of the human settlement.

By allowing these females to escape, Mog made his first really big mistake. This was a major blunder that would come back to haunt him. His foolishness in not having soldiers standing by to kill all human females right away and allowing them to flee the killing fields, cost Mog and his Neanderthals dearly.

Before this terrible day in their lives, most human females had never even dreamed of fighting for their own lives and the lives of their loved ones. Up to this moment they had never considered standing shoulder to shoulder with their male human partners. This had now changed forever.

We all know that there is nothing as fierce as a female lion when she is defending her mate or her cubs. The very same truth applies to our own human females. When Mog badly used, abused and destroyed so many of them on that terrible day of the battle, he caused them to demand and to get what they demanded.

They demanded and got the complete extermination of the Neanderthal race at a later date in time.

Mog's Neanderthals soon found out what it was like to have a female human's deeply rooted hatred, which they inspired in our women on that fateful day. These human women, who were constantly raped and beaten by the Neanderthals, were determined to see the extermination of their hated enemy.

It was the women who absolutely refused to compromise with them to divide up the world between human and Neanderthal as Mog was going to suggest again and again.

It was the women who demanded from their mates, lovers, sons and warriors that they continue the fight until every last one of the enemy was destroyed with no chance of their ever making a comeback.

As we all know, women never forget a terrible wrong done to them and never give up in their relentless pursuit of what is right and proper. This admirable human female trait has not changed over the generations, and we love them for it.

Play nice, play fair and play for real. This is the belief of the modern woman of today who was taught all of these things by their mothers and their mothers' mothers, going way back in the history of our race. This has allowed women to take their rightful place as full partners with their male counterparts in the world of today.

And very soon, if not quite yet, it will be women who make this world of ours a better place for all of us.

T IIⵏ ꜰ T

To be continued …

# ABOUT THE AUTHOR

Bud is the product of Chicago, Illinois. He received his bachelor's degree at the University of Illinois–Navy Pier Branch. His love of history, both ancient and modern, led him to Northwestern University's Special Historical Studies. The terrible Chicago winters found him quickly heading to the warmer climate offered by Southern California, where along with his wife and often co-author, Diane, they moved into a most interesting line of work in and out of several movie studios. For many years, Bud worked as a ghostwriter and story doctor to several famous authors whose names are extremely well known! Bud has teamed up within the last year with the famous second writer for *Gilligan's Island, Scooby Doo, Laverne and Shirley*, etc., etc. His partner's well-known name in the industry is Ron Sellz, and together they have just completed six new novels that should be in print for early 2016. Bud is the father of two and grandfather of seven. Thank you for the read.

www.ingramcontent.com/pod-product-compliance
Lightning Source LLC
Chambersburg PA
CBHW020635260626
47157CB00008B/2748